# By Love
## or
# By Sea

# RACHEL ❧ RAGER

**Bonneville Books**
**Springville, Utah**

© 2009 Rachel Rager

ISBN 13: 978-1-59955-221-7

Published by Bonneville Books, an imprint of Cedar Fort, Inc., 2373 W. 700 S., Springville, UT 84663
Distributed by Cedar Fort, Inc., www.cedarfort.com

LIBRARY OF CONGRESS CATALOGING-IN-PUBLICATION DATA
Rager, Rachel.
  By Love or By Sea / Rachel Rager.
    p. cm.
  ISBN 978-1-59955-221-7
  1. Love stories, American. I. Title.
  PS3618.A379W38 2009
  813'.6--dc22
                        2009002823

Cover design by Angela D. Olsen
Cover art by Alicia Blevins
Cover design © 2009 by Lyle Mortimer
Edited and typeset by Heidi Doxey

Printed in the United States of America

10  9  8  7  6  5  4  3  2  1

Printed on acid-free paper

For my daughters—
Kissing is the best part of the story.
I love you.

# Acknowledgments

Thanks to my mother, sister, and cousin for the extra eye. Thanks to my husband, dad, and brother for all the support and encouragement. I couldn't have done this without you!

Thanks to Alicia Blevins for her wonderful artwork on the cover!

# One

"Is that going to be all for you today, Mrs. Winters?" Alice Lind Frank asked the woman on the other side of the counter of the small dress shop.

"Yes it is, but there's no need to be so darn cheery about it, Miss Frank," the older woman growled.

"I'm sorry you're bent and determined to have a bad day." Alice sighed. "I don't know why you can't enjoy an afternoon like this. After all, it is absolutely beautiful today."

"Ha! That's what you think!" Mrs. Winters sneered at the petite, copper-headed beauty behind the counter. The look of disappointment apparent on the young girl's face fueled the old woman's comments further. "Besides, I don't know why you have to go sticking your big nose into other people's business all the darn time." Tucking her purchase under one arm and grabbing her cane, she hobbled for the door. Opening it, she paused and said curtly, "And for your information, you young whippersnapper, I was having a perfectly good day until I saw your smug face behind that ugly counter." With that, she slammed the door to Alice's nana and pappy's dress shop with such force that a small tuft of dust puffed up from between the planks of the wooden floor.

Alice shook her head in amazement, reflecting on how coldly and unpleasantly Betsy Winters had swept through the dress shop—as though Betsy was the morning frost. Granted, the bitter woman was well into her seventies and probably one of the oldest women in their seaside town, but that gave her no right to treat everyone she saw like they were parasites. Earlier that morning, Mrs. Winters had scowled at the price tag of the dress she wanted to buy.

"Why do you want so much for a lousy dress?" she'd asked.

"The material is of a very fine quality, Mrs. Winters. And lace doesn't come cheap," Alice replied.

"It's ridiculous!" the woman exclaimed. "I won't pay that kind of money for something so drab."

Alice had indeed lowered the price slightly, which undoubtedly Betsy had known she would do. The old woman seemed to run the entire town. Everywhere she went people avoided her like the plague, which seemed to please her. For those who did not avoid her, Mrs. Winters usually succeeded in ruining any happiness they'd had in their countenance previously.

"Was that old Betsy Winters, come to terrorize the world?" Gretchen Lind asked, coming into the main part of the store from the back room where she had been doing some sewing.

"That it was. And she's just as bitter as ever."

"I don't doubt it." Gretchen shook her head and went to retrieve a glass of water she had left behind the counter. "Why, if she wasn't so old, I'd have smacked her flat on her fanny more than once."

Alice giggled.

"Nana," Alice ventured more seriously. "What is it that makes Mrs. Winters such a hostile woman?"

"Well, I'm not real sure. I know she and her husband have been separated for years and years now. But I really don't know much about her," she said before she took a sip of water.

Gretchen Lind was a beautiful woman in her own right. Her once blond hair was now conspicuously streaked with gray and carefully piled on top of her head while her face, though somewhat wrinkled and careworn from age, still glowed with the love for life it had contained in her youth. The blue dress she wore and had sewn herself was simple but tasteful and partially hidden by the lacy apron she always wore when she worked. A sweetheart to the core, Gretchen often had people stop by the shop simply to discuss their problems; she was a good listener and Alice adored that quality in her. Having no sisters of her own to confide in, Alice had loved having a confidant ever since she started living and working with her grandparents.

Alice's own mother, Theresa Frank, worked in the kitchens up at the palace. Alice had grown up in the palace until only recently, and the grandeur of growing up in such a place had always excited her. She had helped her mother with various tasks when the royal family threw balls, banquets, and other special events, but she often found herself standing around, just watching the fancy guests. Alice would often play with the few other children who also lived at the palace. But Alice had always preferred to spend her time with her mother, even though Theresa was a little detached from life. Though a pleasant woman, Theresa had never been the best mother for she often dwelled so much on her own grief and misfortune that she took little notice of her daughter. Still, Alice loved her and had worked with her mother in the kitchens of the palace until almost a year ago when she had grown tired of that life and had finally convinced her mother that she should live with her nana and pappy.

"Oh, I almost forgot!" Alice exclaimed as she nearly ripped the apron from her waist. "I need to leave, Nana. I told Mama I'd meet her in ten minutes," she said, looking at the small clock on the counter.

"Then you'd better run." Gretchen laughed; her granddaughter had again let the time of day slip by her. Alice was a gifted seamstress and wonderful with people, and Gretchen loved the breath of life she brought to the shop. It had been looking so lonely and tired with no young spirit to liven things up. Now with Alice around, the entire store looked as though spring was constantly in season. Gretchen laughed again as Alice, in her haste, nearly ran head long into the doorjamb on her way out the door. Smiling to herself, she returned to the back of the store to finish up a project she had been working on while her husband was out making a delivery.

"I love you, peach. Be safe walking home."

"All right," Alice said, embracing her mother. She turned and started down the road, eager to enjoy the beauty of the day. She had run so quickly to see her mother, she'd not had a chance to revel in the beautiful day.

Stopping at the entrance gates to the palace, she stood admiring the town below. She loved how it sat on a hill overlooking the beach and the shipyards. The shipyards were a quarter day leisure walk from town, but still close enough for all the townspeople to enjoy the pleasure of being near the sea. Surrounding the heart of the town were many farms and to the west of town, the lack of civilization gave birth to the most spectacular meadow filled with beautiful wild flowers. Depending on the season, the wild flowers brushed the grasses with different colors, providing the meadow with a lovely ambiance.

To top it all, as though she lived in a fairy tale, the palace sat on a hill overlooking the town just to the east. The palace had been built a century ago and had several towers. The entire front courtyard was surrounded by archways and pillars. Thousands of statues stood around the palace, both on the building and on the ground; and the intricacy of the stone work, as though the stone had been nothing more than silk in the artist's hands, simply amazed her. Running her hand gingerly over one of the pillars, she marveled again at the soft, cold surface of the smooth, marbled stone. Though somewhat intimidating, it was spectacular to see the structure; as if it somehow protected the quaint little town below. Alice loved the dream of it all.

As Alice began on her journey home and passed through the town, she exchanged pleasantries with a few people but mostly kept to herself, enjoying the view of the vast ocean growing in front of her and the goings-on of the town. Though the town was not large, it bustled with activity. Men could be seen driving teams of horses or helping women and children in and out of carriages. Women were loaded down with packages, wandering from shop to shop or simply standing with other women and gossiping about the latest news. Children ran down the streets, chasing rings with sticks or playing with balls. Alice smiled as one little girl, dragging her doll behind her, tried desperately to keep up with the older children, who seemed intent on deterring her from the game they were playing with a poor dog.

Then, as though nothing more than a mirage, she saw a tired man crest over the hill coming from the beach and walking towards her. The distance between the man and herself allowed her time to stare at him without being obvious. The tall man wore a tattered pair of trousers and a fairly clean, cotton shirt fastened only by three lower buttons, allowing his vast muscles to protrude from beneath as he carried a knapsack on his shoulder. His skin was bronzed from what she assumed were probably years spent in the sun. His sandy whiskers weren't long but had obviously been neglected for many days, and his blonde hair was nearly as white as old Mrs. Winters', but unlike hers, his hair traveled halfway down his back.

He sported an odd appearance, yet he was almost intriguingly familiar. Alice smiled to herself as she speculated about his reasons for being in town and determined he was probably a sailor anchored in town for a few months until his ship sailed again. She loved to see the sailors who came into town—happy, bursting with life, and full of stories from the sea. She imagined this man to be no exception.

As the distance between them lessened, he smiled almost wistfully at her, and she felt herself stop and stare unabashedly at the stranger for, as he smiled, a memory flashed through her mind. She briefly allowed herself to conjure up the image of a boy from long ago. Quickly she pushed the thought away, reminding herself of the impossibility of it. She forced her feet to again continue on their path home. Yet, still staring at the stranger while he passed, she felt the thrill that shot through her body as she saw him wink at her. Finally pulling herself from her constant appraisal of the man, she turned her head back around and continued on down the road.

"Excuse me, miss?"

Alice turned at the sound of a soft, masculine voice behind her and there, looking expectantly at her, stood the man she had been visually devouring only moments before. "Yes?"

"I realize this is probably a strange thing to ask, but . . ." He paused and looked at the inquisitive eyes that were lingering on him from passing spectators. He seemed suddenly less sure of himself. "D-do you know if the . . . the Newman's still live around here?" he asked in a lowered, hesitant voice.

"Well, sure. They've lived west of town about a mile for longer than I can remember." Then as curiosity got the better of her, she could not restrain the question from escaping her lips. "Are you one of Augustus's nephews? You bear a striking resemblance to Augustus himself."

The man chuckled uncomfortably and pushed a hand through his tangled hair. "Well, thank you, miss, but I'm not his nephew."

A look of pain seemed to cross his face before he tipped his head to her in parting and left her alone to ponder on the encounter. Alice knew she had never seen this man before. She would have remembered. His weathered face made him appear quite old, and she felt a stab of sorrow at the look of pain that had so recently crossed his face. The look in the man's eyes caused him to look somehow even older than he did at first sight.

Alice's heart twinged at the thought of what could cause a man such pain. It was a common look among sailors, but it always saddened her. And something about this particular sailor tugged at her heart more than most. Something about him caused her to reflect on a boy from years ago, a boy who had unintentionally stolen her heart. But this man was not he. She would have recognized him immediately. But something in his smile reminded her of. . . . No, she would not think on that. Still, the man did resemble Augustus Newman. Oh, there were exceptions for sure; this man had long blond hair, and Augustus was nearly bald; this man was tall with a strong frame, and Augustus was short and somewhat portly but still very strongly built. Yet she could not get the man's familiar, sad smile out of her head the remainder of the afternoon.

That evening as she sat in the parlor with her nana and pappy, her gaze lingered on the fire while her embroidery sat forgotten on her lap. "What has your mind in a tumble tonight, peach?" Gretchen asked.

"Oh, I don't know," she answered casually.

"Now don't start up with that. I know when something's eating at you, and tonight it looks like whatever it is might just swallow you whole."

"Oh, Nana, you do beat all," Alice said in exasperation.

"I'm serious, peach. Did your mama say something to upset you?" Gretchen pried.

"No," Alice stated simply.

"Well, are you just going to sit there until she drags it out of you, or are you going to tell it to us straight out?" Henry asked, equally concerned about his granddaughter.

"I don't really know what to think, Pappy. My mind's all muddled up and I can't seem to make heads or tails out of any-thing." She loved her pappy. He was a tall thin man with gray hair and high cheek bones. He was a tailor, and Gretchen and Alice helped him out two or three days of the week. He had stepped in after her father had died and had been the only father she really remembered.

"Why don't you start by telling me how things were while you still could make sense of them," Gretchen encouraged.

"Well, I went to see Mama and everything went well. She was attentive to me, and we had a real nice time. I came home, just like I always do and then . . ."

"Yes?" Henry said when she paused.

"Oh, I don't know what to think," Alice whispered desper-ately. "I was walking home, and then there was this man who came over the edge of the hill. He'd obviously come from the beach."

"Was it Clarence?" Gretchen interrupted. "He's normally coming back to town about that time of day."

"Of course not," Henry put in. "She would have recognized him."

Gretchen and Henry were both completely captivated by what Alice had to say, but in truth Alice could not figure out what she was thinking. So how on earth did they think she would be able to tell them a story they could understand? "No, it wasn't Clarence. In fact, I don't know who it was. My gut instinct tells me he was a ghost, except he spoke to me."

"A ghost?" Gretchen laughed. "Really, peach! What would put your mind to thinking something as crazy as that?"

"I'm serious, Nana!" Alice whined loudly.

"All right then. What was it about the man that put it into your mind that he was a ghost?" Gretchen asked repentantly.

"Well, he looked real enough, but he reminded me of . . . He kind of looked like . . ."

"Who?" Henry coached.

"I don't know if I can utter his name." Gretchen's rather disappointed look displayed itself blatantly upon her face. Alice knew her grandparents were dissatisfied with her answer, but she didn't know if she could tell them who the man looked like. So she changed the direction of the conversation. "He spoke to me though. His voice was low and hushed, as though he was afraid to speak."

Once again interested in the conversation at hand, Gretchen asked, "Well, what did he say?"

"He asked if the Newmans still lived around here. And I told him they did."

"Was that all he said?" Gretchen asked.

"Well, no . . . I asked him if he was Augustus's nephew because his face bore such a striking resemblance to him. But he said he wasn't."

"Peach, Augustus doesn't have any nephews. He's an only child," Henry interjected.

If Augustus was an only child, was this man's resemblance to Augustus simply one of those bizarre, coincidental things? Or could he possibly be. . . ? No, certainly not. Going over the situation out loud made no more sense than it had in her mind.

"Alice, who was it that the man reminded you of?" Henry asked.

"Pappy, I don't know if I can utter his name," Alice whimpered.

"And why not?"

Alice hesitated, attempting to give enough information without actually having to say the man's name aloud. "He died about six years ago in a ship wreck while he was at sea as a merchant sailor."

"Are you trying to tell us that you spoke to Caleb Newman on the street in town today?" Gretchen asked reverently.

"I don't know that it was him, Nana. And besides, how could it be him? Remember? Grace said there were no survivors."

"But . . ."

"No, Nana. I'm certain my mind was just playing tricks on me. It was probably some poor sailor, anchored in town for a few days." With that, the topic died, and the conversation moved on to other things, but that night as Alice lay in bed waiting for sleep to engulf her, the image of the man on the street kept her weary mind company. He was, after all, intriguing and very striking in his appearance, no matter how tattered and tired he looked. The thought of him being an older version of the ever-so-handsome Caleb Newman made the mystery of the man all the more enticing. He had been such a good looking young man; tall and very handsome. Rolling over with a smile on her face, she eventually found respite as she fell asleep thinking of the young man she'd thought of so often before.

After meeting with the red-headed beauty on the street, the

weary sailor made his way aimlessly down the old, familiar street. The petite girl had unsettled him, which is why he had stopped her. She looked as sweet as a sugar stick. He had needed a few more moments to study her, for she had reminded him of someone, a girl he had known as a young man. It had taken him less than a minute to determine that this girl, whoever she was, was a rare piece of work. Her eyes boasted the color of the amber setting sun, and her hair claimed the color of deep copper that danced with fire in the dying light of day. With freckles sprinkled delicately across the nose on her perfectly porcelain complexion, her face beamed with an obvious love for life. Years had passed since this man had seen someone with such a rare beauty about her.

Shaking his head he dismissed the thoughts of that girl and turned his mind and attention to the task at hand. As anxious as he was to make this visit, nerves dominated his being. So many years had passed since he had seen this family, yet some unseen force seemed to be propelling him onward. He always imagined his soul would rejoice when this day arrived. It had played out in his mind so many times, but now he was concerned. Concerned for the heartache of the Newmans and concerned for how this meeting would affect them. Down the main street of the town he walked and out past the town to where the farmers had their land.

The man rounded a corner and continued his journey until finally his gaze fell upon a little, cream-colored cottage with lush green trees framing the yard and a few flowers growing along the pathway, which led to the door. He frowned at the appearance of the old cottage, for a visible sadness seemed to engulf the entire property. Instead of the flowers exhibiting the colors of vibrant pinks, reds, and dark purples, all the flowers were white or pale and blended in with the cottage. The neatly trimmed grass was infested with the sprinkling of weeds, and only part of the fields behind the house held corn while the rest had been taken over by weeds and briars.

A heavy sigh escaped his lips as he thought of the suffering these good people had undoubtedly gone through. Before he could reconsider, the weary sailor began the long walk up the pathway to the house. He had intentionally waited until late afternoon to set out for the house because he knew that by the time he arrived, both Augustus and Grace Newman would most likely be in for the night, and he needed to talk with both of them. As he finally reached the door, he set his knapsack on the ground beside him and, with much trepidation, raised his hand and knocked loudly three times before letting his hand fall to his side. He had no choice left to him except to endure the torturous silence before the door opened.

Finally, the door slowly opened and an aging woman, nearing sixty, looked questioningly at the man who stood on the other side. The sailor felt the tears sting his eyes before they silently spilled onto his cheeks at the sight of the woman. Her once rich, dark brown hair was now silver and white. There were circles under her eyes, as though she hadn't slept in years, and her countenance was gloomy and sad, as though her spirit had died. Suddenly the woman gasped and clasped a small hand over her mouth, shaking her head and trying to stifle a sob.

The man could hold back no longer and choked out, "Hello, Ma."

Grace approached him hesitantly with tears streaming down her careworn face. Tentatively reaching out, she placed a dainty hand to his darkly tanned cheek and gazed deeply into his cobalt blue eyes. "Caleb?" she whispered, as though she were afraid he was only a memory and would disappear again if she spoke any louder. "Caleb? Is it really you?"

"Yes, Ma. I'm home." An instant later he found himself in her loving arms, and they stood there holding each other, crying. He had dreamed of this tender moment nearly every night for many years. His mother's love filled him with such a feeling of acceptance and healing, he was astonished at the joy he experienced. There was only one thing missing. "Where's Pa?"

"Oh, he went out to the barn for something. He should be back any minute." As she looked at her son who had grown into a man, the twinkle that had been lost from her eyes before partially returned, but some clouds seemed to loom in them as she asked, "What happened to you? They said you died that night of the wreck. How'd you survive?"

Caleb looked around before he answered her. "Do you mind if we sit for a bit? I've been traveling all day, and I'd like to tell you and Pa at the same time."

"Whatever you say, honey." she smiled as she took his hand and led him to the parlor. The woman's happiness radiated from her as though she had just witnessed an angel. Her countenance beamed with delight, and Caleb knew that she had suffered greatly in his absence.

After they were seated, Grace on the couch and Caleb in a chair across from her, Grace's joy seemed to heighten as she continued to look at her son. "Well, you've certainly filled out right nice. You look just like your daddy when he was young. But your hair's awful long."

"Yeah." Caleb chuckled, self-consciously pulling it away from his face and behind his shoulders. "I was kind of hoping you'd cut if for me before I go into public again. People stare at me like I'm a leper."

Just then, the kitchen door opened and Caleb heard heavy footsteps on the floor as his father knocked the dirt off his boots as had always been his habit. "Hey, Gracie!" came Augustus's voice from the kitchen. "Do you have some more of that old material we used to tie around the poles out west of the barn to mark those baby trees? We forgot some this morning and I want to get them done quick-like before I forget where they are."

"Augustus, we've got company. Can we do it in the morning?"

"Well I suppose so," he said. His footsteps were heard leaving the kitchen and moving towards the parlor. "And who is it that's come a-calling at this hour?"

The back of Caleb's chair faced the doorway of the parlor, and Caleb knew his father wouldn't recognize him from the back. So standing, he turned around to greet Augustus. Upon entering, Augustus looked first to Caleb, and then to his smiling wife and back to Caleb before the realization seemed to set in. "Son?" he croaked. He reached out for the wall to keep him upright. Augustus was a short man with very little hair atop his head, and the hair that was on the sides was mostly gray. His tan and careworn face sported stubby whiskers from not shaving since the early hours of the morning, and his eyes glistened with moisture as he caught sight of Caleb standing in the parlor.

"Hello, Pa. I'm home," Caleb whispered. He went to his father, his emotion caught in his throat, and quickly embraced him.

Pulling away momentarily, Augustus said, "But I don't understand. How can this be?"

"Well, he wanted to tell us both together, so stop your blubbering and come have a seat. The suspense is near to eating me alive," Grace said. Though what she said sounded a bit harsh, both father and son chuckled knowing her obvious eagerness to hear the story.

Only one thought entered Caleb's mind as he walked back to his chair. It was good to be home. He had missed his mother's theatrics, her gentle manner, and her generosity. He'd missed working alongside his father and Augustus's ability to make him laugh. So many things were wonderful about home; he never wanted to leave. And yet, he wondered how long he would be able to stay.

"All right, don't get your corset strings tied in knots." Augustus chuckled as he made his way to the couch next to his wife, and Caleb moved back to the chair he'd occupied only moments before. "So, tell us, son," Augustus began, more seriously as he took his wife's hand in his. "Wasn't it your ship that sent all aboard to meet their maker?"

"Yep, the Blue Sparrow did get shipwrecked like you must've heard about ten months after we set sail. And from what I've gathered from talking with various people, there weren't any survivors." That's what everyone had told him about that ship—no survivors. He looked down guiltily at his hands as though he had never seen them before; those hands that served him in so many ways and ultimately had saved his life.

"No survivors, except me," he choked out in an emotional whisper.

"So what happened? How'd you survive?" his mother asked.

Swallowing the lump that had unexpectedly formed in his throat, he lifted his eyes to his mother's. "I don't know," he stated simply. "I got knocked unconscious by a giant wave, but not before I'd secured myself to a beam and that must have helped save my life somehow." He quickly looked at the expressions on his parents' faces. The horror of what had happened to their boy was all too apparent on their faces, and Caleb's heart ached for the burden his disappearance caused them. "Shortly after I washed up on shore, I joined up with a crew sailing east. I had to stay with them for five years. And then it's taken me nearly a year to get back home."

Yes, that's what happened; or at least the bare details of what had happened. He wasn't sure he would ever be able to tell anyone the entirety of his story. This explanation should suffice, he told himself again. It was all anyone ever needed to know about his seven years spent at sea.

"Why didn't you write?" his mother asked.

"We seldom if ever passed a ship coming this way and were almost never on land."

"Does anyone, then, know you survived?" Augustus asked.

"Before I came here I stopped in and saw Anthony Hielott. Actually his son, Clarence, was in the office but as I was leaving I met up with Anthony. He offered me his apologies for what happened, not that any of it was his fault, and he told me he'd help in any way he could to get me on my feet again."

"Well, that was nice of him," Grace said.

"Sure was. He was very helpful to us right after it all happened. He's a good man, he is," Augustus replied.

Silence followed Augustus's comment as the family sat staring at each other with grins on their faces. Each person lost in his own thoughts, yet each one thinking the same thing. It was good to be together as a family again.

"Are you hungry, honey?" Grace finally asked, breaking the silence. "I've got some leftover stew in the kitchen."

"That sounds good. I can't remember the last time I had a real good hearty meal, let alone homemade," Caleb said. He stood and followed his mother into the kitchen.

As Grace tended to Caleb and made sure he had plenty to eat, Caleb and Augustus talked of the farm and the town. When Grace finally sat down, Caleb asked, "Whatever happened to Jameson Thatcher?"

"He works for old Bailey down at the livery," Augustus said.

"He married yet?"

"Nope. You know how shy Jameson is. He pretty much stays to himself," said Augustus.

"But I think he has a girl over in Charleston County he sees quite frequently," Grace added, and Augustus nodded.

This news pleased Caleb. Jameson was a good man and deserved to be happy. "Are the Linds still in town?" Caleb asked.

"Yep," Augustus said. "Your mama goes over to visit Gretchen from time to time."

"And you remember Alice?" Grace said and Caleb nodded slightly. "She's living with them now. She's such a pretty girl and all grown up," Grace said conspiratorially, and Caleb did not miss the look of warning that his father threw her direction.

Caleb ate quietly for a few more minutes before he spoke again after wiping his mouth clean. "So, whatever happened to the Burns? Are they still around?"

Grace and Augustus exchanged glances before Augustus answered. "They're still in that house down the road, if that's what you're asking."

Caleb nodded. "And what of Lydia? Did she marry that Spencer what's-his-name?" he asked sarcastically.

"Yes, Caleb, she did," his mother said gently.

Caleb continued eating, staring into his bowl of stew in order to conceal his reaction. Over the past several years, he had become proficient at covering up his true thoughts and feelings, no matter how deeply they affected him. "Hmm, well, good for her," he stated matter-of-factly.

"I'm so sorry, Caleb," his mother soothed.

"What for?" he countered nonchalantly. "It's not your fault my ship sank in a storm and everyone thought I was dead. I certainly didn't expect to come back and see her sitting around becoming an old maid because she was so heartbroken over my death." But he also hadn't expected to find Lydia married to Spencer Tollwhite.

"Now she didn't mean that, son," Augustus said, trying to mend the bridge before it burned down completely. "She only meant—"

"I know. I'm sorry. I guess I'm just tired," he said, guilty for his behavior.

"Let me get you a warm bath, change the sheets on your bed, and then you should get some shut eye," Grace said as she stood up from the table.

"Thanks, Ma."

Caleb was still somewhat stunned at both seeing his parents and actually hearing someone say that Lydia married Spencer Tollwhite. Caleb had imagined she married someone, but it was still difficult to hear it spoken. She had been angry to learn of his leaving but by the time he left, they had parted as friends. So for her to have heard of his death had most likely been shocking or even devastating. She had evidently turned to Spencer for comfort and support. Who could blame her? Caleb certainly didn't. He was uncertain he would do any different if the situation had been reversed. Though his thoughts and feelings towards Lydia had never been what she or anyone else had thought they were or should be, she was still a sweet girl and only deserved the best. He prayed that Spencer endeavored to deserve her.

As he lay in bed thinking of so many different things and experiencing so many complex emotions, his mind wandered back to the red-headed beauty from town. His countenance lightened some as he pictured her; copper curls flying in the breeze and her face flushed from the fresh air. Perhaps she was the Linds' granddaughter. The thought encouraged him, for she had been a delightful little girl. He remembered meeting her for the first time—red hair escaping her two pig-tails and wearing a white pressed apron while carrying a tray of fruit at a royal ball. Even at such a young age she had been able to cause his heart to flip-flop with excitement. They'd spent many days together those first years and she had enchanted him, yet she had been entirely too young for him. Still, she'd be grown up now and he briefly allowed his mind to linger on the girl from his boyhood. Was she the same girl he'd met in town? Whoever the red-headed girl was, she probably had a fiery temper and would look simply adorable with her petticoats tied in knots. *Maybe,* he thought as he drifted into a fitful slumber, *maybe I'll test it out sometime.*

# Two

A week had passed since the unsettling stranger made his first appearance in town. Since that time, the neighbors had bombarded Alice with questions about the odd-looking man in town. On the day she'd spoken with the tattered yet alluring sailor, she vaguely remembered people gazing at them while they conversed. But now it seemed as though everyone was invading her private moment with the mysterious and intriguing man. Everywhere she went people wanted to know everything about him from who he was, to where he came from and what words he'd exchanged with Alice. Of course there were speculations of all kinds about his identity and what a man of his obvious upbringing was doing in their town, but no one really knew for sure. No one, Alice suspected, except the Newmans.

When asked what the stranger had said to her, Alice simply said, "He asked if I knew of any good barbers around." True, it was a lie, but she was not sure this man would want people poking their noses where they didn't belong, especially where the Newmans were concerned. So, she continued to tell her lie and hoped that soon enough the truth of his identity would be revealed.

On this beautiful summer morning, Alice found herself at the local general store along with none other than the ever bitter Betsy Winters. As Alice entered the building, she could tell before anyone said a word to her that something had already gone awry. She quickly looked around and found Mrs. Winters hunkering over a basket of paints and sifting through them almost carelessly. Smiling at Nancy McCullam, the store keeper, Alice approached the counter.

"Good morning, Mrs. McCullam."

"Good morning to you, dear. How is everything today?" the woman said, feigning a pleasant tone.

"Very well, thank you. It's a glorious morning, don't you think?"

Before Nancy McCullam was able to say anything, Alice heard a muffled noise of disagreement coming from Betsy Winters, which she had expected. "I'm sorry, Mrs. Winters. What did you say?" Alice asked cheerfully, despite Nancy's head vigorously shaking back and forth in warning.

"I didn't say anything to you, child, and you'd do well to keep out of others' business," Betsy grumbled without turning around.

Alice heard the bell to the door of the general store ring, indicating someone entering the store, but she did not turn to see who it was. At this particular moment she had a thing or two to say about Mrs. Winters' terrible attitude. "I beg your pardon, Mrs. Winters," Alice countered pleasantly, putting on her best manners in order to infuriate the old woman even further. "I only approached you because you made such a disgusting noise. So I assumed you meant to enter the conversation."

Now the older woman turned on her heel to face Alice. Alice had evidently hit a tender chord in the woman's heart and smiled pleasantly at the frown that was ready to do battle with her. *Hit me with whatever you've got,* Alice thought. She determined that the beauty of the day would not be tarnished for her by the likes of Mrs. Betsy Winters.

"What kind of brat are you that you'd dare speak such things to a crippled old woman? Didn't your mother teach you to respect your elders?"

"Yes, Mrs. Winters, she did," Alice answered, trying to stay calm at the mention of her not-so-attentive mother. "But you are not crippled, and I don't feel I need to respect someone who doesn't respect me or anyone else around her," she finished contentedly.

"You!" the woman hollered and Alice saw Mrs. McCullam take several steps backward as she watched the argument taking place in her store. Several other patrons also seemed to have gathered around to witness the confrontation. "How dare you!" Betsy said, taking a step towards her opponent and pointing her cane at the girl as though ready to joust. "You think you know so much, don't you, with your lacy dresses and your nose sticking up through the clouds. Well, let me tell you a thing or two. There's nobody who I'm going to let run me like a stupid mule. So don't think I'm going to heed anything you say to me. But I'll tell you this little missy. If you don't stay out of my way—"

"Then what?" Alice asked with a mocking laugh. "Are you going to turn me over your knee? Well let me tell you a thing or two, Betsy Winters," she began more seriously, and almost heard more than saw the raised eyebrows of everyone in the room at the mention of the older woman's full name being used so informally. "First of all, next time you speak ill of my mama, I'll knock you into the next town. Second, there is no one in this town that owes you a darn thing, so you need to get that thinking out of your mind. And third, I will get in your way any time I want because I'm the only person in this beautiful town who's not afraid of you, and I'm tired of you being so sour you turn the milk bad every time you pass a cow. So, if you don't want to enter into a conversation with me, I suggest that in the future you keep your mouth closed."

Alice smiled inwardly to herself as she felt many pairs of eyes boring into her and saw just as many mouths gaping open in surprise. She then turned to Mrs. McCullam, as though the confrontation with Betsy Winter's had never occurred, and said, "Here's my list, Mrs. McCullam. Nana just needs a few things today. I hope it's not too much trouble." Nancy McCullam took the list tentatively from Alice though her gaze remained on Betsy

Winters. "Is something wrong, Mrs. McCullam?" Alice asked. Nancy shook her head and hurriedly disappeared to take care of the girl's list. Alice looked back to Betsy Winters as though she had just noticed the woman for the first time. "It certainly is a beautiful day, isn't it, Mrs. Winters," she ventured cheerfully.

The older woman simply grunted and took her leave. As the door to the general store closed behind the woman, Alice suddenly burst into laughter. Mrs. McCullam appeared again and looked at the girl in surprise. "My goodness, child. I thought she was going to eat you for lunch."

"Betsy Winters? Get the better of Alice Lind Frank? Over my dead body." Alice laughed as she turned to look at some books.

She stopped dead in her tracks, however, and the color faded from her lovely face instantly when she turned around and saw, for the first time, who had entered the store at the beginning of her confrontation with Betsy Winters. There standing before her was Grace Newman and the sailor Alice had met only a week before. But today, the sailor stood tall and erect and looked rather amused instead of defeated. Today his hair was cut to a neat length while his freshly shaved cheeks revealed a slightly rounded but healthy face with high cheek bones and soft features. The man looked much more approachable than she had originally thought. Her gaze traveled over his face, and his eyes seemed to capture hers. She noticed his eyes sparkled with something that had been absent on their previous meeting: happiness, peace, love.

Her feet remained rooted to the ground as she stood there staring at the man; her mind playing tricks on her again. There was no plausible reason this could be the man he appeared to be. Was there? She had seen that face so many times before but only now did realization dawn upon her. This man's image had haunted her dreams for thirteen long years and only now could she put that face with a name. Oh, she had longed for the man in her dreams to be that boy she had once loved but could it really be he? Impossible.

She continued to gawk at him, and her mind whirled.

The man smiled, and she fought desperately to keep her tears restrained. Who was this man? And why? Why did her mind plague her with the memories of that boy from so long ago? She was happy now. Her life was just as she had planned it that night after. . . . Yet she found herself wanting this man to be that boy. But . . . why was this all coming up now?

"Good morning, Miss Frank," the low sultry sound of the handsome man's voice rang out.

"Uh . . . good morning, Mr. . . . uh . . . sir. Mrs. Newman," Alice managed to say in greeting to the pair.

"Good morning, Alice. Do you remember my son, Caleb?"

Alice could feel the lightheadedness begin to settle in as she began to sway just slightly. "Of course," she finally choked out. It really was him!

She saw the smile spread across Caleb's face. Then she heard the shuffle of feet and muffled voices as the room started spinning and going fuzzy. A moment later, her knees gave way, and everything before her went dark.

"I hate to say it, Gretchen. I expected as much from most people, but certainly not from such a confident girl as Alice."

"I know. And I can't for the life of me figure what made her do it."

Alice slowly came out of her unconscious state. Looking around, she saw that the voices belonged to her nana and Grace Newman. Upon further evaluation she concluded that she lay in the spare bed in the back room of her grandparent's store. Carefully, she began to sit up, arousing the attention of the older women. "Are you all right, peach?" her nana asked.

"What happened?" Alice managed to whisper.

"Well, after your encounter with old Grouchy Winters, which you should be hailed for, I might add, I introduced you to my son, who's just come back from sea, and you simply swooned."

Grace's expression of confusion seemed to match Alice's own confused state. "If it hadn't been for Caleb's quick feet, I'm afraid you might've hit the floor pretty hard."

"So it wasn't a dream?" Alice ventured. "You mean he really is back?"

"Of course, darling," Grace affirmed with a smile.

"And isn't it wonderful?" Gretchen sang joyously, and Grace nodded in agreement.

Alice rubbed at her chest trying to make the frantic beating of her heart slow to normal. "And how did I get here?"

"Why, Caleb brought you, of course. I wasn't about to let you stay there for anyone to come in and see your weakened state," Grace said, motherly-like. "Can you imagine what old Betsy Winters would say? Or those two Whitmer sisters?"

A thrill shot through Alice's body at the thought of being carried in Caleb's arms. The sight of his strong bronze arms would undoubtedly cause any girl to swoon. But Alice had been held in them. Of course, she was unconscious at the time, but she could almost feel their strength beneath her now. "Is . . . is Mr. Newman still here? I'd like to thank him for . . . for helping me," Alice stammered.

"Oh no, darling. He had to go get some hardware for our gate. The wind's managed to blow it off its hinges again," Grace said, shaking her head. Seeing the look of disappointment on Alice's face, she continued, "But I think he's planning to attend the social with us tomorrow evening."

Alice smiled, for she knew the woman was merely trying to please her and put her mind at ease. Thinking of seeing Caleb at the farmer's social tomorrow caused her heart to leap before she quickly scolded herself. The farmer's social was when the farmers and some of the locals in the county got together to have lots of food, games, and dancing. Generally the wealthier did not attend these activities, but Alice always thought they were exciting. "Thank you, Mrs. Newman, for your trouble. I'm feeling much better now."

Grace smiled at Alice then turned around and said, "Now

Gretchen, you let this girl come by the house soon so we can have us a little chat."

Alice didn't miss the quick wink the two women exchanged, but she had no time to comment.

"Well, I'd best be off," Grace said. "I don't want one of those Whitmer girls hounding my Caleb." With that, Grace blew Alice a kiss and left.

"What have you two been talking about while I've been out of it, Nana?"

"Don't you go worrying yourself over not knowing everything there is to know." Gretchen smiled warmly at her granddaughter. But as she stood looking at her, the smile changed from warm and affectionate to sympathetic and lamentable. Carefully, Gretchen sat on the bed next to Alice and cupped the girl's face with one hand. "He is the one, isn't he?" she finally asked softly. "The one in your dreams."

Gretchen said it as fact, as though she already knew the answer. Yet Alice still nodded her head solemnly in awed agreement. "What does it mean, Nana?" she said with tears spilling onto her flushed cheeks.

"I don't know, peach," Gretchen said. She quickly pulled her into an affectionate embrace. "I don't know. But don't worry. You'll figure it out."

"Hello there, beautiful." At the sound of the masculine voice, Alice looked up to see Caleb coming straight for her. Upon arriving at the farmer's social in the meadow west of town, Henry headed off to visit with some of the men while Alice and Gretchen were seized upon by Grace. In fact, Alice had just finished hugging the woman when she heard Caleb's voice. Not having seen the man since she'd fainted in the general store yesterday morning, she felt both embarrassed and thrilled that his attentions landed upon her. As he approached, her gaze fell momentarily to his strong arms, the capable arms that had carried her to safety yesterday morning. They were well hidden beneath the sleeves of his shirt, but she could still imagine his amply defined muscles beneath the cotton softness.

As Caleb came towards the women, he threw a quick wink and smile to Alice before turning his attention to his mother and giving her a hug. "Hello, honey." Grace laughed as Caleb picked her up and set her back down again. The thought occurred to Alice that perhaps Caleb had directed the affectionate greeting towards his mother, and her cheeks burned with an uncomfortable blush.

"So," Caleb said, after he released his mother. "Are you ladies ready to have a good time?"

"Would we be here if we weren't?" Gretchen asked.

Caleb laughed before his gaze fell upon Alice. "I'm glad to see you're feeling better, Miss Frank."

"Yes. I'm quite well, thank you," she said cordially. "And thank you so much for your assistance yesterday in saving me from further embarrassment."

Before Caleb could answer, Alice saw his eyes narrow and then she felt a warm hand at her waist. "Hello, Miss Frank," a deep voice said.

Alice smiled and turned around to greet the man who belonged to the voice. "Hello, Clarence," Alice said happily.

A thin man of average height, his hands had obviously never worked a day in the fields. With strawberry blond hair, eyes the color of the sea, and a smile that could charm anyone, Clarence Hielott was the most sought after man in the county. His skin was fair without a freckle, but his face sported a scar that began between his eyes, traveled to the left of his nose, hooked under his cheek, and followed his jaw line to his ear. The scar had been quite ugly at one time but now it was simply a line that added definition to his face.

"What are you doing here with that man?" Clarence whispered in her ear before placing a lingering kiss on her cheek.

Gretchen loudly cleared her throat, causing Alice to pry her attention away from Clarence before she could answer. Then Gretchen said as sweetly as possible, "Caleb, this is Clarence Hielott. His father owns Hielott & Son. Clarence, this is Caleb Newman."

"Yes, we were acquainted in our youth and met again briefly the other day at the office, I believe," Clarence said.

"Yes. Your father owned the ship I used to sail on. Great man, your father," he said placidly as he offered his hand to Clarence, who accepted it briefly.

Clarence smiled while eyeing Caleb suspiciously but said nothing at first. "Are you the one who survived the shipwreck of the Blue Sparrow?" Alice could feel the unspoken tension that hung ominously in the air between the two men even though their words were polite enough. Alice had gone on a walk with Clarence several nights ago, and Clarence had neglected to mention seeing Caleb. She sensed there were unresolved issues between the two.

"I am," Caleb said calmly, although Alice could see his eyes narrowing again as he looked daringly at Clarence.

"Well, I'm glad you returned home safely," Clarence said, trying to dispel the tension in the air as best he could. Then turning to Alice, he asked, "Shall we dance, Miss Frank?"

"Certainly," she said, smiling at him. She allowed him to escort her to the dance floor that had been erected on the meadow floor especially for the occasion, but she couldn't help catching the blatant look of disapproval that crossed Caleb's handsome face.

"What were you doing with the likes of that man?" Clarence asked after he and Alice started dancing. He attempted to sound casual, but Alice saw possessiveness in his eyes.

"His mother and Nana are good friends, you know that. He simply came over to see his mother."

"And that's all?"

"Of course. Why?"

"Well, I heard of your little incident yesterday and so naturally I assumed—"

"What?" she challenged.

"I was merely wondering why you fainted dead away in the general store after you'd already encountered him earlier in the week."

Alice looked at him in bewilderment. "I . . . I thought he was dead. When I met him on the street, I didn't know who he was. He was just a worn looking sailor. And . . . and then yesterday in the store . . . it was just a lot to accept and take in."

"What was so difficult about it?"

"What was so difficult?" Alice repeated angrily, trying to push the tender emotions from her voice. "He was supposedly dead for six years and then he saunters back into town!" Alice stopped abruptly as she realized people were beginning to look over at her. "I'm sorry if I didn't handle it as well as everyone else," she finished more quietly.

Nearly in tears from Clarence's intense scrutiny of her attitude towards the new man in town, she simply wanted to leave and have herself a good cry. But Clarence pulled her to him in a reassuring embrace. Embarrassed at how close he held her while still dancing, she pushed away from him smiling as an indication that she was feeling better, when in reality she had no desire to see any more of Clarence Hielott the remainder of the evening.

At the conclusion of the song, Clarence escorted her from the dance floor; while he went to visit with someone, Alice found herself momentarily alone. Seeing Gretchen talking with Nancy McCullam and rearranging the pies on the refreshment table, she nearly headed over there when Grace took up occupancy at her side. "Well, what do you think?"

Hesitating, Alice answered, "About what?"

"Anything! The beautiful night, the dancing, the food, Clarence, Caleb . . . all of it. What do you think?"

"It's a bit overwhelming," Alice answered honestly.

"How so?"

"I don't know," she paused. "I . . . I guess . . . I just didn't expect. . . . It's just not what I planned."

"What do you mean by that?"

Smiling, Alice reluctantly told the woman some of what plagued her mind. "I thought he was dead. And now he's back and . . . Clarence, I imagine, will be proposing to me any day ,and I don't know what to tell him. I should say yes, but what if . . ."

"Alice, you need to follow your heart," Grace said knowingly.

"I know, but I don't know what it's trying to tell me. I've loved your son from a distance my entire life."

"I know," the woman replied so softly the girl didn't hear it.

"But he's always loved someone else and has never even seen me. He always. . . . I hardly know him. Why should I wait for something I know in my heart will never happen?" Alice mused aloud; she had almost forgotten she had an audience. Her mind began to play out the scenarios that had plagued her for a week now. The many possibilities of what might happen if he did find an interest in her. Would he sweep her off her feet? Would he kidnap her and marry her? Or would he simply confess his undying love to her and profess that he could not live another minute without her in his life? Highly unlikely.

She told her heart that the childhood longing she once held for him was foolish and she knew from experience that nothing good would come from wishing it. Still, a part of her longed to be held in his arms and kept safe. She wanted to hear him whisper her name lovingly into her ear. But would it be worth the disappointment and heartache that would inevitably follow when he lost interest in her?

Then there was the issue of Clarence, who had been paying her court for nearly five months. Always a perfect gentleman, he flattered her endlessly, and she found herself enjoying his attentions. Even though she had been unsuccessful in allowing herself to love him, she knew he was a well-mannered, industrious man and that he would provide well for her future. She would never want for anything.

Still . . .

"Don't worry. It'll all work out," Grace said, bringing Alice out of her thoughts. "And don't feel like you have to do something because it's what someone else wants. Do it because it's what you want." Then Grace gave her a quick squeeze on the arm and, with a wink, left Alice to her thoughts.

Later that evening, Alice found herself sitting alone on a small hill overlooking the party. She smiled at the young and old couples dancing. The old women sat talking on one side of the platform and the old men sat on the other while the young people sprinkled in between. She had always found a strange sense of joy watching others dance, and tonight proved no different. The stars sparkled and danced across the sky to the music. The laughter floated through the air on the light breeze of this peaceful evening, and she smiled at the excitement everyone exhibited.

Clarence never left her side throughout most of the evening until a friend of his, Richard Forkworth, took him away on some business matters. Richard, she knew, had been friends with Clarence since they were young and now worked for Clarence. He looked the part of a sailor, tall, darkly tan, and with dark hair. He had always been kind to Alice, though he seemed quite shy and didn't say much; still, he had a way of intimidating her. Clarence explained this away by pointing out her unfamiliarity with him, and Alice accepted the justification without question.

Now as Alice watched everyone, she saw Jameson Thatcher cross the dance floor with a beautiful brunette, whom Alice had seen only three times before. Jameson had been a friend of Caleb's as long as she could remember and from what she had witnessed this evening, they were evidently still good friends. At the next moment, she witnessed Caleb cross the floor with a girl. Alice's heart sank to the bottom of her stomach as recognition of the girl dawned on her. Lydia Tollwhite. Lydia and Caleb had been friends since they were young and had courted the year before he left for sea. When word came that Caleb's ship had sunk, it had been common knowledge that Lydia was devastated, though she married Spencer Tollwhite just a few short months later.

Alice felt the jealousy burn inside her as it had done so many times already that evening; every time Cora or Sally Whitmer danced with him or any other beautiful girl for that matter. But why? Why was she so jealous? She awaited a marriage proposal any day from a very handsome and productive man. Yet she didn't want him. Or did she?

Laying back in the clover and looking at the stars as the song ended and a new one began, her head continued to swim with questions of her future. She enjoyed Clarence's company, and he was a good friend but something about him had never sat well with her. Although it was nothing tangible, something always kept her from getting as emotionally involved with him as he obviously was with her. Then unexpectedly, Caleb showed up and sent her head and heart into remembering things that were nearly forgotten except in the loneliness of her dreams.

Closing her eyes, she attempted to block out the memories that threatened to come into her mind, as had been their habit nearly every night since she was six. *No!* Alice's mind screamed. Those memories and the pain. The humiliation. She could not deal with it now. *No! Please, not tonight!*

"No," she muttered under her breath as her head rocked slowly from side to side.

"No what?"

Alice sat up instantly as her eyes shot open, and she looked around to see who had spoken to her. Everything spun as the result of sitting up so quickly, and when the world stopped spinning she saw him. Caleb Newman stood looking down at her with curiosity evident on his handsome face. "What are you doing here?" she asked curtly.

"Your Nana asked me if I'd seen you. So, figuring you were missing, I came to find you," he said as he sat down beside her.

"You came to find me?" she asked. She looked at him in wonder and curiosity. *Why?* Alice wanted to know.

"Yep," he said as he began to chew on a blade of grass and looked out over the crowd below them. "Are you enjoying yourself tonight?"

"I guess. You?"

He laughed and she tried to suppress the smile that was

threatening to spread across her face at the beautiful sound. "I haven't seen so many girls vying for my attention in so long. It's kind of funny."

Instantly the smile faded from her face. "Yeah, a real delight," Alice said sarcastically.

"Now what are you so sour about tonight, Miss Frank?"

"What's it to you?"

"Well, I came up here to ask you for a dance, and you're just being plain rude."

Taken aback slightly she said, "Do you always speak your mind so, Mr. Newman?"

"Always." Something clouded his expression but vanished so quickly she thought she must have imagined it. He turned to her and, quirking one eyebrow, said, "So how about that dance then, Miss Frank?"

Alice paused with reluctance for only a minute before she slowly nodded and allowed him to pull her to her feet and lead her down the hill to the platform. The touch of his hand sent an unexpected thrill up her arm and through her body; she nearly yanked her hand from his, for the sensation greatly unsettled her. Memories of him from her childhood had overwhelmed her mind all evening, but as he held her hand in his, he suddenly became tangible. No longer was he simply a memory or someone she had always adored from afar. Now he stood before her, holding her hand, smiling, and leading her to the dancing couples below.

The idea of him being so close, though exciting, terrified her. He was the ideal man in her eyes and always had been. As the thought entered her heart, however, the heartbreak she had endured at his hand quickly squelched any thrill she had experienced previously. She reminded herself of his haughty demeanor and arrogant air. Undoubtedly he had changed very little in seven years. And she had no desire to be on the receiving end of his self-important character for longer than a short dance. Her heart would not be destroyed this time. Thinking such thoughts steeled her for the pain she would otherwise endure as she walked like a lamb to the slaughter with her assassin.

Upon reaching the platform, Alice and Caleb stood silent with their arms linked, waiting for the song to finish and a new one to begin when Cora Whitmer approached from behind and clasped Caleb's free arm. "Mr. Newman," Cora cooed. "Would you like to escort me to get some pie? I know how much you adore cherry pie."

Caleb smacked his lips and winked at Alice a second before turning his attention back to Cora. "You know I do, Miss Cora. But I promised the next dance to this lovely girl you see hanging onto my arm."

Alice smiled triumphantly. Cora Whitmer prided herself in her charm and never ceased to use it on unsuspecting and handsome men. Alice thought the girl's charades usually made her appear quite foolish and shallow. Still, the thought of capturing Caleb's attention away from Cora made Alice happy to the core.

"Aren't you engaged to Clarence Hielott, Alice?" Cora asked, feigning sincerity.

Alice's face turned red, and she fought to remain in control of her temper. "No, but I'd appreciate it if you kept such jealousy in check."

The song ended then, and Caleb led Alice to the platform, leaving Cora gaping at them both. Waltzing with him, Alice had a difficult time separating her previous emotions from her current ones, which helped to fuel her aggravation. "That Cora Whitmer boils my blood," Alice said.

Caleb just laughed. "Maybe you just let her get to you too easily."

"Now why would I do that intentionally?" she countered.

"I don't know. Why did you accept the invitation to dance with a stranger if you're promised to another man?" he said more seriously, yet careful to conceal the thoughts from his eyes.

"I'm not promised to him, nor am I engaged to him. And you're not a complete stranger."

"True. But you two looked pretty serious to me. Tell me something, why would a pretty little girl like you let a snake like Clarence Hielott anywhere near you?"

"What does it matter to you?" she snapped, hurt that he still saw her as a child.

"Does it bother you that I asked?" he arched a single eyebrow, a characteristic Alice had always adored.

"No, I just don't see how it's any of your business," she said flatly, trying to focus her mind on Clarence as opposed to her dreamy dance partner.

"Let me ask you something. What do you see in old scar face anyway?"

"He's very attractive," Alice started.

"Yeah, like a snake," Caleb said, sneering.

"Will you let me finish?"

"Sorry." Caleb nodded for her to continue.

Alice started again, "He's attractive, very attentive to me, and loves me very much." She nodded in satisfaction. That should stop any questions Caleb could throw at her.

Caleb's crystal blue eyes bored into her amber ones. At that moment, his eyes cleared and the guarded intensity they held earlier disappeared as he briefly let down his defenses. "Do you love him back?"

"What?" she asked breathlessly, not sure she heard him correctly.

"Does he make you laugh?" Caleb asked. He nearly stopped dancing with her but did not let go of his firm yet tender hold of her.

"Why?" Alice breathed deeply as tears started to fill her eyes. "Why would it matter to a selfish, conceited person like you who or where I choose to place my affections? You've never cared one smidge if I were dead or alive. So why would it matter to you now?"

Caleb stood there, shock radiating from his handsome face, and she could see the hurt in his eyes as they clouded again to cover his emotions. *Let him be hurt,* she thought. That was the very pain she'd experienced at his hand nearly every day for the last ten years. Tears began to spill down her cheeks, and she could no longer endure his gaze. Humiliated, she turned and ran for the safety and solace of the small hill, where she remained until her nana and pappy were ready to leave.

"How did you enjoy the social tonight, honey?" Grace asked her son after they arrived home and retired to the parlor. Caleb had worn a constant frown on his face since his dance with Alice, and it concerned Grace. After a short while of their almost dancing in the meadow—and Grace considered it almost dancing because they hardly moved, rather they had stood there holding each other and arguing—Alice ran off, and it had taken a half hour for Henry Lind to find her. Not only that, but Caleb had refused to dance with anyone else the remainder of the evening.

Shrugging his shoulders Caleb said, "It was fine. There are some mighty fine people around here."

"What did you think of Alice Lind Frank?" Grace asked as she received a reprimanding look from her husband.

"I don't know. She's not real willing to let anyone near her. That's about all I've come up with. I didn't talk to her for long."

"But—"

"I'm real tired, Ma. I'm off to bed." He gave her a kiss on the cheek, nodded to his father, and disappeared down the hall.

Disappointment filled Grace. She knew Alice could do better than Clarence Hielott, but she also knew the girl had issues concerning Caleb. At the same time, she could see the longing in her son's eyes when he looked at Alice, and she wondered briefly what might be holding him back. Shaking her head and sighing loudly, Grace slouched, most unladylike, back in her seat.

"Don't get your petticoats wet over it," Augustus said with a wink. "It ain't over yet."

# Three

The following morning, Alice found herself on a small ladder picking cherries from the trees in her grandparents' backyard. She looked forward to this time each year. Even when she lived with her mother at the palace, they had often come to pick cherries to take back to the palace for a few pies. Alice loved cherry pie. She liked the flaky crust her mother made and the delectable cherries in the middle. Her mouth began to water as she thought of the tart, ruby red morsels of fruit she picked. Yes, put a little cream on a hot piece of cherry pie and Alice was suckered in. But cherries were loads of work. First, they needed to be picked from the tree, a time-consuming process in itself. Next, they were sorted and pitted, if they were to be canned and put in pies; or they were simply juiced for jellies and syrups. Cherries were a great deal of work, but well worth every effort.

Henry and Gretchen Lind had nearly an acre covered with cherry trees. There were so many cherries that they usually sold most of them to the general store. Today and tomorrow, Alice, and perhaps her mother, would pick the cherries the Linds would keep. Then, Henry would pay some local boys to come over and help pick the rest so they could be taken to the general store to be sold or Alice and Gretchen could turn some of them into jellies or syrups to be sold in town or given away as gifts. The entire tedious process bore rewards that were plentiful, and

Alice enjoyed it immensely.

As she reached up again to pluck another handful of cherries from their resting place on the tree, she heard the cracking of a branch. She knew cherry trees generally were not sturdy enough to climb high into so she kept most of her weight on the ladder and used the tree limbs more for balance. But as the cracking noise reached her ears, she quickly twisted to see how badly the limb had split. To her horror, she lost her balance and went tumbling off the ladder. When she landed, she realized she had been caught by someone before knocking them both to the ground. Picking herself up and smoothing out her skirts, she stopped short when she saw Caleb, now stretched out on the ground with his head propped on his hand, eating a cherry.

With a satisfied smile on his face, he mumbled, "Well, I'll say this about you. You certainly have terrible balance."

"That's not true. I thought the tree was going to snap out from under me," she countered.

"A twig snapped under my boot. And you have terrible balance." He chuckled and spat the pit on the ground near him.

She knew he spoke the truth. She lost her balance all the time, but she would never admit it to him. "What are you doing here?"

Standing, Caleb brushed the grass from his pants. "Ma sent me by to pick some cherries," he said, indicating some buckets on the ground beside him. "Gretchen said they are ready for picking, and since Pa and the boys were just doing some light stuff around the farm today, Ma sent me over."

"Nana said you were working down at the shipyard."

"Not today," Caleb said with a triumphant grin.

"I see," Alice said grumpily. She did not feel like spending the day picking cherries with him, especially after what she had said last night. "Well, there's another ladder over by the house," she said pointing, and then headed up her own ladder again to continue the tedious task. She wasn't certain his company would be pleasant to have. Picking cherries got lonely at times, but she wasn't sure she wanted *his* company.

Oh, the tumultuous emotions he could stir within her! He could cause her to feel elated, jealous, angry, and whimsical all within a few minutes of each other. Granted, he probably enjoyed pushing her buttons but, oh, the emotional ride it took her on. Yet no matter how angry or upset she was with him, he still managed to make her heart quicken, her stomach flip with excitement, and her mouth water with a coveted longing for his kiss. Realizing her mind lingered on the thought of his kiss, Alice scolded herself inwardly and resumed her task.

When Caleb returned and started picking cherries, he spoke to her again. "So what have you and old scar face been up to this week?"

"Must you call him that?" Alice sighed with exasperation. "He is every bit as much of a man as you or anyone else."

"Right," came his sarcastic response.

"Just because he has the constant reminder of a painful mistake from his childhood doesn't mean—"

"A painful mistake?" Caleb repeated in disbelief as he stopped picking so he could turn and look at her. "Do you even know how he got that hideous thing?"

"Yes," Alice said with some slight hesitation in her voice. She peered at Caleb skeptically. "He slipped by the cliffs east of town as a young boy."

"Let me guess, that's what he told you." When Alice nodded, Caleb shook his head and rolled his eyes in disgust. "Of course it is. The weasel can't even fess up to his own stupidity."

Caleb continued his chore of picking cherries while muttering something under his breath Alice could not hear. His ladder nearly touched hers, though he cleaned a different tree of its beautiful fruit. Glancing over at him, she noticed his head was almost level with her own for, while she stood perched on one of the top rungs of her ladder, he'd stopped on a much lower one. She watched as he picked the red morsels of fruit. He wore his shirt, but it hung open revealing his chiseled chest beneath. The forehead of his handsome face puckered in a frown and a sudden desire arose within her to reach out and smooth it back to its natural form.

"What?" he growled, noticing her obvious scrutiny of him.

She jumped slightly. Regaining her composure, she asked, "Will you tell me what really happened?"

"With Hielott?" When Alice nodded, Caleb let out a long sigh, set his bucket on a ladder rung, folded his arms across his massive chest, and, leaning against the ladder, began his tale. "I don't know how old we all were, maybe about ten or so. . . . I can't remember for sure. I never knew him very well. He's always been a snake in the grass, so I always kept my distance. One day something will happen to that snake, and I want to be as far away from him as I can." Caleb rubbed his freshly shaved chin, a dark expression clouding his eyes briefly.

"Anyway, a bunch of us boys were going out to the old warehouse down by the beach for a little bonfire one night. Well, Clarence's folks said he couldn't go because they were having company over for supper. We told him we'd be there until sundown and to come when he got done. Evidently, he did something to make his parents send him to his room early and then he snuck out his bedroom window."

Alice listened to the story intently. It was strange to think Clarence had never elaborated on the circumstances surrounding the event before, especially since they had spoken of marriage. It made her momentarily wonder what other things he had withheld from her. Those thoughts were pushed to the back of her mind, however, as she stood listening and staring at the heavenly built man who stood just a short distance in front of her. Her insides fluttered with desire as she was able to study him so closely without being questioned.

Caleb stood looking at her but not seeing her as he continued the story. "It was nearing sunset when he finally snuck out, I guess, and instead of going down the road to the beach, he decided it would be faster to climb down the cliff wall." Alice's eyes widened in disbelief, and Caleb finally saw her and laughed mockingly. "I know. Dumbest thing I ever heard. Clarence's always been like that too. Always looking for the fastest, easiest way to get whatever it is he wants. Bypass everything in the middle, unless it will give him gain."

After a couple minutes passed in silence, Alice finally shook her head and said, "So how did they find him?"

Caleb had resumed his cherry picking and when Alice asked her question, he did not stop as he gave his answer. "Well, the story goes that later that night, Anthony went to check on him and found the window open and no Clarence. So Anthony went over to Jameson Thatcher's and asked him if we'd seen him. We, of course, hadn't. He probably fell as we were coming home from the beach. So Anthony got a search crew together, and they set out looking for him. Pa was out helping them and said they found him about six feet down from the ledge around midnight that night. The boy was too much of a weakling to even pull himself back to the top."

"How awful that must've been for poor Clarence," Alice mused aloud.

Stopping his task, he turned to look at her in dismay. "Poor Clarence? What about his parents? They were the ones who had no idea where he'd gone off to."

"I know. But Clarence had to stay there for hours, his face all cut up and waiting for someone to find him. It's probably amazing he didn't die from infection."

Caleb looked deeply into her eyes before reaching over and cupping her face with his hand. His hold on her face was uncomfortably firm. Yet Alice was amazed at the hot, tingling sensation that permeated her entire body from his touch. It sent her heart racing and the butterflies twirling in her stomach. His face hovered so close to hers, she fancied she could almost feel his breath upon her lips. Then, ever so provocatively, he nearly whispered with barely restrained anger, "Tell me something, Miss Frank. You don't really buy into his farce, do you?"

"I . . . I don't know what you mean," she said indignantly, trying to appear unruffled by his handling of her.

"I mean, do you believe everything he's ever told you?"

"Well, I've never had any reason to doubt him."

As she watched his face contort with concern, Alice felt

compassion for the man. They had once been good friends, and he undoubtedly only wanted to look out for her. Grateful to him for wanting her happiness, part of her wanted his concern to be for more intimate reasons.

"I don't know that my heart has believed it all," she amended in a whisper.

"That's very nice to hear," he said grinning, all evidence of annoyance gone.

Her eyes opened in astonishment as her attention suddenly became arrested by his tongue gliding effortlessly over his lips, cleaning some cherry juice from them. The action, though innocent, caused her mouth to water for sudden want of his kiss. Then his hand left her face and traveled down her neck where it rested as his thumb caressed her face ever so tenderly. "So then, sugar, did you miss me while I was at sea?"

Alice was stunned into momentary silence. It had been years since he had called her sugar. In fact, he was the only one who had ever called her sugar and it had been far too long since she had heard it sung beautifully over his enticing lips. Yet, the name carried with it a bittersweet collage of memories. It not only reminded her of the association they'd shared from so long ago, but also the hurt and pain that accompanied that association. The thought stung and she fought to gain control of her emotions once more. "I don't . . . I . . . I thought you were . . ." she breathed.

"Shhh. I'm back now," he said, putting a hand to her mouth to silence her while caressing her lips lovingly.

"Stop teasing me," she hissed as tears started to fill her eyes, for she knew, just like before, that he could never be hers. The pain of that knowledge caused her heart to ache.

"I'm not teasing you, sugar. You know, I thought of you while I was away those many years," he said softly. "You were such a cute little thing."

"Don't try flattery with me," she said angrily and suddenly pushed him away from her. He nearly toppled off his ladder. Alice couldn't believe he'd succeeded in doing it again. They'd been sharing pleasant conversation and then the inevitable—his teasing turned to mockery. Again. He was still the same conceited, obnoxious boy he'd always been, and she remained merely a servant girl. Seriousness always evaded him, as though everything was a game. Stepping down from the ladder she spat, "It's always the same with you, isn't it? Tell me, Mr. Newman, did you come here just so you could set my temper aflare? Because if you did, you're about to get one whale of a show."

"Now come on, sugar. You know I'm in earnest," he said, following her as she marched away from him.

"Is that so?" she said turning to confront him. "Then why did you try telling me you've thought of me over the years? We both know that's not true. You were so hung up on Lydia Burns, you never saw another girl. Did you?" Caleb said nothing; he only looked down at the ground guiltily.

Alice marched angrily away once more.

"Alice, wait," Caleb called, running to catch up with her. Grabbing her by the arm and causing her to turn, he put both hands on her shoulders. "I did think of you while I was away. Honestly. I had a dream about you one night several years back and thought of you more and more as time went on. So many times I'd try and imagine what you'd look like all pretty and grown up."

"You really expect me to believe that?"

Gradually, as she allowed herself to look at him, she began to feel sorry for him and wanted desperately to believe him. Her anger disappeared and was replaced with pity. He looked tired and defeated, and it almost broke her heart. She turned, hoping to distance herself from him so she wouldn't make a sudden fool of herself because of her softening heart. However, her attempt to flee was thwarted as a strong arm wrapped protectively around her waist and turned her into Caleb's tender embrace. She looked up into his crystal clear blue eyes that twinkled with amusement as the shock from the situation danced in her own eyes.

His free hand brushed a loose strand of copper hair from her face. "Yes. I want you to believe me. I need you to believe me. And I want you to think of me the way I've been thinking of you." He leaned forward and gently placed a light kiss on her cheek. His kisses then traveled down her neck and to the hollow of her throat. The sensation his kiss evoked within Alice caused her knees to buckle, and she melted against his body like honey on a hot biscuit. She closed her eyes and threw her arms around him, drowning in the euphoria his affections bathed her in. When he stopped, she was finally able to find her wits again, and she slowly opened her eyes, silently pleading with him for his kiss. A smile spread across Caleb's face as he read the longing in her eyes. "Can I kiss you?" he whispered.

Nodding affirmatively, Alice closed her eyes and waited with anticipation. In the next instant Caleb's lips met with hers in a hesitant and delicate kiss. Knowing he'd undoubtedly been deprived of female attention for many long years, it thrilled Alice that he chose to place his affections on her and that he chose to do so in a gentle manner instead of a ravenous, wild beast. Her heart had dreamt of this moment for thirteen long years, and he proved to be more magnificent, even in this tender exchange, than she had ever dreamed.

As their kiss continued and began to intensify, she felt her arms go up his back until they felt something under his shirt. The skin on his back was raised from an injury of some kind. She traced the wound through his shirt and it seemed to extend from the top of his shoulder blade to the middle of his back.

Caleb broke their kiss with a light gasp and pulled her arms around him to rest on his arms. "It's a little sore there," he whispered, as he endeavored to again start up their interlude.

"But what . . . ?" Alice tried to say in between his soft kisses.

He broke away long enough to whisper, "It's not important. Just kiss me."

As he began to kiss her anew, she found herself swept away in the passion of the moment, oblivious to all else. Oblivious to all the birds chirping happily in the trees, the breeze whispering ever so softly, and the door slamming shut. *The door!* Alice promptly pulled her mind to the present again and spun around to see her pappy leaving the house. He descended the porch stairs with his head bent down. Maybe he hadn't seen them; at least, she hoped he hadn't. She heard Caleb chuckle behind her as she stood rooted in place and watched as Henry approached.

"How's it going out here?" Henry asked innocently.

"Pretty good, sir," Caleb said. Alice turned to see that he again stood on a ladder picking cherries, and she momentarily wondered how he'd gotten there so quickly.

"Good, good. Well I'm off to work," Henry said. "Just wanted to get a quick kiss from my girl."

Alice instantly wondered if he'd seen her and Caleb seconds before, but when she looked at his face, she saw no sign of his teasing nature. So she smiled and gave him a kiss on the cheek. "Bye, Pappy. Have a good day!"

"You too, peach. Now you go pick me lots of cherries so we can have us a cherry pie tonight." He smiled at her and gave her a pat on her seat as she went back to her ladder.

Henry Lind laughed to himself on his way to the shop. *Now that's the kind of kid she deserves,* he thought. How Alice had ever hooked up with Clarence Hielott, he'd never know, but Caleb Newman was a good kid and would treat her well. From what he saw, Clarence treated her well too, but he didn't deserve her. Catching Alice sparking with Caleb among the cherry trees only moments before had been a welcome sight. He chuckled to himself as he thought back on the instant he'd chosen to leave the house. After the interlude he'd witnessed, he hadn't wanted to embarrass his granddaughter or the boy, so he made no mention of their previous activities. Henry was sure Caleb knew he'd seen them or at least had a heavy conscience. The boy scurried back to the ladder quicker than a hornet flying to its nest, as though he was trying to avoid a switching. Henry simply laughed. No harm ever came to anyone who did a little kissing among the cherry trees.

"Do you think he saw us?" Alice unintentionally spoke aloud her thoughts after Henry left.

"Most likely. Why?" he asked, quirking one eyebrow up at her in question.

She shook her head slightly as she returned to her ladder to resume picking cherries.

"Do I embarrass you?"

"No. . . . I mean, yes . . . I. . . . Maybe. . . . I don't know," she stammered as her head stumbled to sort out her confusing emotions. Her heart still soared at the mere thought of Caleb and his kiss. Yet she was nearly engaged to another man. Not only that, long ago she had sworn she'd never fall for a man like Caleb. In fact, Caleb had forced her heart to come to that decision in the first place. As a result, the very thought of their interlude confused Alice.

"It's all right, sugar," he said, smiling sadly. "I understand." He stared at her from across the ladders, and she saw pain flash through his eyes. She longed to know the source of his pain and what had caused it. Was it the painful memories of another woman? Or pain from her unwillingness to reach out to him? She obviously had good reasons not to simply reach out and take him as her own but was it possible something held him back as well? Or did his pain stem from something else entirely?

As she studied his countenance, a shadow passed over his face, and he appeared to be momentarily lost in thought. Finally, after a long minute of silently contemplating each other's deliberation, he spoke quietly, as though the question pained him to utter. "Sugar, why did you quit talking to me all those years ago?"

Just then, Alice's attention was drawn to the back door as

Gretchen exited, carrying more buckets and several large bowls. Alice sighed, feeling guilty yet grateful that she could postpone the answer to Caleb's question.

"I thought I'd come out and do some pitting while you both picked," Gretchen said cheerily. "I'm not interrupting anything, am I?" Gretchen asked looking from Alice to Caleb.

When Alice posed no comment, Caleb offered, "No, ma'am. I was just telling Miss Frank that I think Ma will be along shortly."

"Will she now? Well, she's always a breath of fresh air, now isn't she?"

Alice giggled as Gretchen practically skipped back to the house for two chairs for the women to sit in. Alice's heart swelled with gratitude that Gretchen and Grace would be pitting the lush cherries. That was the worst part of the job in Alice's eyes. She loved to pick the cherries and loved turning them into jellies, syrups, or pies but wanted nothing to do with trying to get the pits out of them. The sticky, tedious chore almost seemed like a waste of time as far as Alice was concerned.

A glottal noise coming from the direction of her picking companion caused her to turn her attention back to the man who had recaptured a piece of her heart moments before. She saw a smile dance merrily across his handsome face and felt the butterflies dance madly within her bosom. "You and me, sugar, we'll finish this little chat sometime soon, you hear?" She nodded as he climbed down the ladder and moved it to another position around the tree where more cherries awaited him.

The remainder of the day was spent in laughter, fun, and buckets and buckets full of cherries. Alice and Caleb continued to pick cherries while Gretchen and Grace sat nearby pitting the seeds and putting the fruit in the bowls. The constant chatter from the two older women the entire day occasionally enticed Alice or Caleb to join in but as far as holding a conversation together, it did not happen again that day. However, Alice did catch Caleb staring at her a time or two but when she did he would simply smile and throw her a playful wink before resuming his job.

That night, Alice retired to her bed, tired and sore from reaching up to pick hundreds of cherries. She knew yet another day of picking awaited her and as her head hit the pillow, she looked forward to the following day. Even in her exhausted state, while her mind slipped into unconsciousness, her last thoughts were of Caleb. His smile. His wink. His touch. His kiss.

## Four

*Knock, knock, knock,* Alice's hand sounded confidently on the door a few evenings later. She knew she would have to keep her wits about her. This was a risky thing to do. She stood poised on the porch with a warm cherry pie in her hands. How could she be refused? Even by someone as sour as . . . "Mrs. Winters. How nice to see you this evening," she greeted cheerfully.

"What in tarnation do you want?" the woman said, sneering.

"Well, Nana and I were baking pies today, and I thought you might like one."

"And what devil would you possess to make you think a thought like that?"

"Do you like cherry pie, Mrs. Winters?"

"That's no business of yours," she growled.

"Then I'll just leave it here on your porch for the birds and insects," Alice retorted.

"Now that's the devil talking, it is. What kind of person would irritate an old woman so?"

"Can I put it on your counter for you then?" Alice asked, pleased that her previous comment had worked the way she'd hoped. The woman grunted and moved aside so Alice could enter. The cluttered mess of the woman's home surprised the girl as she entered. She briefly wondered what Betsy did all day long. With no husband, no job, no garden, and no children to look after she probably had nothing to do all day. Yet her house looked as though she had a million things to attend to—except her housework.

"Just put it over there," Betsy directed to an empty spot on the kitchen table.

Setting the pie down and looking around, Alice said, "I don't mean to be nosy, but could you use some help straightening some things up in here?"

"Well, you are nosy. A nosy little brat. And I don't need your help or anyone else's." The woman looked upset and offended. Alice imagined that no one had ever ventured to approach the old woman's home before for any reason. "You've done what you came for, now leave," Betsy said.

As Alice left Betsy's home and the door slammed shut behind her, she vowed to somehow help the woman by being her friend. Whether she wanted one or not.

"That was a pretty brave thing you did, Miss Frank," she heard as she descended the porch steps. She knew the voice belonged to Caleb before she even looked up to see him. "Most people would have rather hung to their death."

"I'm not most people," she replied easily.

"I know," he said, as he came to stand in front of her. "Boy, do I ever," he said with a sly grin.

"Now what do you mean by that, Mr. Newman?" she said, throwing her head to the side and flirting a little with him as she began walking towards her grandparents' home.

"Only that my lips have been watering for yours ever since that day in the cherry grove, sugar," he said.

She stopped walking to look at him in amazement. By the grin on his face, she knew he only wanted to tease her, but the look in his eyes indicated that perhaps he was also very serious. "Tell me, how long have you dreamt of my kiss? Only just recently? Or longer than that?" he asked softly.

"What would make you pose such questions, Mr. Newman?" a deep voice said from behind Caleb, before Alice could answer.

Dusk had dawned and with it grew the difficult challenge of seeing, but Alice would have known that voice anywhere.

"What do you want, Hielott," Caleb said, rolling his eyes and turning to look at the other man.

"I want to know what you meant by that inappropriate comment towards my fiancée," came the reply.

"I am not your fiancée," Alice said perhaps a little too loudly and quickly. Both men quickly turned their gazes to her. Caleb's face held surprise mixed with triumph while Clarence's face contorted with hurt and restrained anger. "I. . . . Even though we've spoken of it, it has not yet been decided one way or the other," she amended quickly.

"Well, if that's the case," Caleb said casually. "Then my comments were not so inappropriate," he said with a grin towards Clarence.

"From now on you will keep your distance from the girl, Newman."

"And why is that? Is she another fine piece of property that you've illegally acquired?"

At such a brutal allegation, Alice watched Clarence carefully for his reaction. Clarence seemed unfazed in spite of the comment, and turned his attention to Alice. "Miss Frank, will you allow me to escort you home?" he asked as though Caleb did not even exist.

"Of course," she said with a smile and took Clarence's outstretched arm. One look at Caleb, however, and she wondered again what ill feelings these two held for each other. "Good night, Mr. Newman," she said. He tipped his head to her and watched as she walked away with Clarence.

When they were almost to the porch, she couldn't help but ask, "Why would Mr. Newman make such harsh accusations towards you?"

"I have no idea," Clarence said. "The only thing I can figure is that he's jealous of what I have." He smiled at her and she blushed slightly.

As he stopped on the porch, he gazed lovingly at her. "You

are the most beautiful woman I know, Miss Frank."

"Thank you," Alice said as she looked down at the ground. He showered the compliments on her far too frequently, but she was too polite to refute them. "Thank you for walking me home."

"You're welcome. Will you be available for an outing tomorrow evening?"

"I think that would be lovely," she replied with a smile. She couldn't help but admire his gentlemanly ways. "Good night," she said and turned to enter her grandparents' home.

Walking to the parlor, she found her nana working on her needlepoint and her pappy reading a book. "Did Betsy like the pie?" Gretchen asked.

Alice shook her head to clear her thoughts. She had almost forgotten that she had originally gone to take a pie to Betsy Winters. "Oh, I think so. At least I got in the door and left it on the counter."

"Good. Did Caleb walk you home?"

Alice looked briefly to her nana who sat eager for an answer while her pappy seemed immensely engrossed in his book and ignorant to the conversation at hand. "No, Clarence did," Alice replied.

"Oh. Well, Caleb stopped by looking for you."

"I did see him, but Clarence met us and walked me home."

Gretchen nodded and seemed to absorb the information before returning her attention to her needlepoint. "Well, that's nice."

"I'm going to bed," Alice said and went to give her nana and pappy a kiss good night. "Good night," she said, leaving the room.

"I have heard mention that you and Mr. Newman were acquainted in your youth," Clarence said as he led Alice down the quiet street the following evening.

"Yes."

Clarence seemed to wait for her to elaborate, but she continued to walk by his side in silence. "How did the two of you meet?" he finally asked.

"Oh," she said, surprised by his sudden interest in the topic. "I . . . I don't really remember."

"I see. Did you see him often as a child?"

"My nana and his mother are friends, so I suppose I saw him on a few of the occasions I spent with my grandparents."

Clarence nodded thoughtfully. "Do you know why he . . . ?"

"I actually am a little confused as to why we are speaking of him at all," she said, interrupting his question. It unnerved her that he would probe her with questions regarding Caleb in the first place. "Surely you know him better than I and are much more aware of his shortcomings. So, is there really any reason to interrogate me further as to my knowledge of the man?"

Laughing, Clarence squeezed her arm lightly with his hand. "My dear, Miss Frank, I only wanted to assure myself that you are more interested in me than the new man in town. Though, I have noticed you harbor some fascination towards him. I was merely testing your reactions to my questions in order to see where your true attentions lie."

"I can assure you, Mr. Hielott, that I do not place my affections or my attentions dishonestly."

Clarence smiled but made no further mention of Caleb Newman or any related topic the remainder of their time together.

Late into the night, however, Alice lay in bed, unable to fall asleep. She kept thinking back to the strange way in which Clarence had spoken of Caleb. Was it true that he was simply jealous of the other man's attentions towards her, or was there an ulterior motive for Clarence's comments?

Suddenly, she heard a faint pounding on the front door, startling her. Jumping from her bed, she grabbed a wrap from the foot of her bed and rushed out of the room to see who was at the door. Opening the door, she screamed as Caleb stumbled into the room and collapsed on the floor in a lifeless heap. The sight of him caused her heart to pound. With all her might, she rolled his unconscious body over and gasped when she saw the state of dishevelment he was in. Kneeling beside him, she gently examined one of his bloody hands. A tear escaped her eye as she noticed that his left eye was turning purple, one side of his lip was cut and swollen, and he had blood caked all over his face. Seeing more blood on his shirt, Alice ripped his shirt open and gasped at the bruises that were already appearing on his body.

"You're pretty bold to rip off a man's clothes, sugar," Caleb groaned in a whisper, struggling for air.

"Stop teasing me," she scolded softly and wiped another tear from her cheek. "Who did this to you?"

"What's going on out here?" Henry asked as he emerged from his room buttoning his shirt.

"It's Caleb!" Alice exclaimed, standing. "He's badly hurt."

"Caleb! Boy, what have you done this time," Henry scolded. Caleb began to cough, and Henry looked deeply concerned. "Gretchen!" he called.

Gretchen was behind him nearly the instant he called. Upon seeing her, Henry stepped out of the way to allow Gretchen space to do her doctoring. "Henry, go get some cold water from the pump. We need to get the swelling down," she ordered. Then kneeling down to Caleb, she said, "How do you feel, honey?"

"I've lived through worse," he commented hoarsely.

Caleb began to cough once more, and Gretchen said urgently, "Alice, go get me some cloths and a blanket to put under his head.

Alice darted down the hall in a panic. Would Caleb be all right? Who had done this to him? And why had he teased her so about having lived through worse? Did he not realize the seriousness of his condition? Her mind was whirling so quickly that she did not realize she had passed the linen closet until she was in her room. Hurrying back down the hall and throwing open the cupboard door, she retrieved the blanket and cloths to clean him and raced back to assist Gretchen.

Upon her return, she realized that Gretchen and Henry had moved Caleb to the parlor, and she entered without hesitation, rushing the cloths to Gretchen. "What happened to him?" Alice asked. She began to help her grandmother bathe Caleb's body. One look at him and she assumed he had either passed out again or fallen asleep, so she looked to her grandparents for answers.

"Nearest that we've gathered, he was leaving Anthony Hielott's place and was set upon by three big fellas. After those hounds left him to weather the elements, he made his way here because it was closer than his folks' place."

"Who were they? What did they want?" she asked.

"Don't know," Henry said with a shrug. "Caleb didn't recognize them. But it looks like he gave a good account of himself, the way his hands are beat up."

An hour later, Gretchen and Alice finally had Caleb cleaned up and resting on the couch; Henry had gone to the Newman's to let them know of Caleb's condition. Caleb, it seemed, would be fine, though Gretchen suggested he might be sore for a few days. But he had no broken bones, and with the exception of a few bruises, he was no worse for the wear; just exhausted.

Alice went back to her room and climbed into her bed. She was worn out from the events of the night. She had worried for Caleb the entire time she and Gretchen labored to clean his body from the blood and dirt. And even though he appeared to sleep comfortably, she still worried about him.

As she snuggled down under the blankets, Gretchen came into her room and sat down next to her on the bed. Gretchen smiled lovingly at her and asked, "Tell me how you feel about him, peach."

"Caleb?" Alice asked. When Gretchen nodded, Alice shook her head slowly and closed her eyes as the tears began to roll down her cheeks. "I don't know, Nana. One minute I hate him for all the things he's ever done to me, and the next minute I'm melting under his briefest touch."

"Has he kissed you other than just the other day in the cherry tree grove?" Instantly Alice looked at her nana in surprise. "Your pappy saw the two of you and told me," she explained.

Shaking her head again, Alice said, "No. It was only that one time." Then staring out the window to the stars, she said, "But so much of the time I find myself dwelling on it and longing for the moment again." Turning back to Gretchen suddenly, she asked, "Am I completely ruined, Nana? I don't love Clarence. I never have but I do have strong feelings for him that may one day grow into love. I have even considered marrying him. Then Caleb comes back from the dead, and everything I vowed to myself all those years ago starts to seem less important and begins to fade. Yet I can't let go of the hurt from the past. The pain. The humiliation." She closed her eyes again and another tear leaked out the corner of her eye. "Am I a complete lost cause, Nana?" she whispered.

"No, peach. I think you're just in love."

"But Nana, I can't be. I just can't! Not with *him*!"

"And why not?"

"Because . . . because . . ." Alice couldn't find the words she wanted. Perhaps there were no words to explain what she was feeling; why she could never again be in love with Caleb Newman.

"Just rest, peach. You'll feel better in the morning." Gretchen gave her granddaughter a kiss on the forehead and, leaving the room, left the door open a small crack.

"How's she doing?" Alice heard Henry ask Gretchen a moment later. She strained her ears so she could hear the conversation taking place down the hall.

"She's confused but I think she'll figure it out," Gretchen replied.

Silence filled the night for a minute. "That's a good boy in there," Henry said finally and Alice assumed he spoke of Caleb. "I wish he knew who'd jumped him and I'd take out after them."

"Yes. It'd just tickle me pink if he and Alice . . ."

"I know," Henry affirmed.

The music floated gently through the evening air as six-year-old Alice Lind Frank sneaked out the palace's kitchen door to look in on the breathtaking ball being held in the next room. She loved to watch the aristocrats dance in their fancy clothing, listen to the beautiful music, and even snitch chocolate covered strawberries when her mother's back was turned. Beauty and elegance graced the palace tonight for the wedding anniversary of Prince Lawrence Phelps and his beautiful wife, Princess Lillian. The couple looked exceptionally elegant, as did the entire royal family, and Alice giggled as she fancied that one of the young men dancing with a young girl was smiling at her.

All around her, marble statues guarded the candelabras that lined the ballroom. Fifteen small chandeliers hung majestically from the vaulted ceiling, surrounding a much larger one in the center. In the candle light, the crystal pieces on the chandeliers sparkled like tiny diamonds glittering in the night sky. The floor of the ballroom was patterned and designed with various colors of marble and had been polished until it shone like a mirror. The white marble pillars along the walls were carved with many shapes and contours, and while Alice had lived here her entire young life, she had yet to discover all the stories they told. At the front of the room sat two beautiful, hand carved, wooden thrones. They had been artfully crafted out of walnut by the late queen's cousin, and the intricacy of their designs emulated the love and admiration for those who sat on them. Alice had dusted the thrones earlier that day and knew that they were as smooth as folds of silk and just as breathtaking up close as they were from her current position clear across the room.

"Alice, come back inside," Theresa Frank exclaimed with a sigh, for probably the tenth time in the last hour. "Here," she said giving the girl a tray of fruit. "Take this out to the table and bring the empty one back. Do you think you can manage that?"

"Yes, Mama," the young girl replied. But as Alice began to

walk into the ballroom, her eyes fixated on the dancing couples, and she stopped to gaze at them. Everyone appeared to be having such a good time. People were laughing, smiling, dancing, and talking. It simply delighted her young eyes to behold such gaiety and she briefly wondered what it would be like to attend a royal ball as a guest instead of a servant.

Then, as though out of a dream, a young man, who she guessed was about thirteen, began to approach her—the same boy that had smiled at her earlier. Alice noticed his handsome good looks instantly and gazed at him, intrigued. Bleached blond hair, probably from being in the sun all the time, adorned his tall and somewhat lanky body. But his beautiful, charming smile and sparkling eyes captivated Alice's attention.

"Can I help you with that, little miss?" the boy asked.

She gazed into his crystal blue eyes, eyes she knew she would never forget. They held mischief in them which radiated into his magnificent smile. She nodded and allowed him to take the tray to the serving table where he placed it in the empty tray's place. He set the empty tray on the ground near the serving table before he grabbed a chocolate covered strawberry, smiled at her, popped the entire thing in his mouth and turned back towards the dance floor. After he left and she finally got her wits about her, Alice ran up behind him and pulled on the tails of his dress coat to get his attention. "What's your name?"

"My name?" he asked as he turned back around to look at her. "I'm Caleb Newman. Lillian's my cousin." Alice nodded as she tried to file the newly learned information into her head. "And who might you be, sugar?"

"My name is Alice Lind Frank. My daddy's a butler and my mama and I work in the kitchens."

"Well, I guess you'll be wanting this back then, won't you?" he said as he picked up the empty fruit tray and held it out to her.

"Yes, sir," she said politely and took the tray. "I have to get back now or Mama will tan my hide. But if I see you again, may I say hello?"

"Of course, sugar. Just say the word and I'll be there," he said as he brushed a strand of her unruly copper hair away from her face.

Alice looked up at the boy with a huge grin on her face before turning and skipping back to the kitchen. He was the most handsome boy she'd ever laid eyes on *and* he'd talked to her. Elation filled her. And because he was Princess Lillian's cousin, Alice would surely see him again. The remainder of the evening, Alice went about her work cheerfully and occasionally went to the kitchen door to make sure the handsome Caleb Newman still graced the ballroom with his presence.

Alice smiled to herself as she awoke momentarily from a fitful sleep. She'd always loved that memory—the first time she'd met Caleb. Instantly, she got out of bed and made her way down the hall to the parlor. Caleb still slept soundly on the couch, and Alice breathed better when she saw that he was, in fact, still breathing. Making sure he did not have a fever, she returned to her room. But as her head again hit the pillow, she began to fade into unconsciousness and desperately tried to fight off the memory that would inevitably follow. *No!* she tried to tell her subconscious. *No, I can't stand it.* But as was so often the case, her tired, weakened mind lost the battle, and the memory came anyway.

Three years ago tonight Alice Lind Frank had first met the ever-so-handsome Caleb Newman, and she had been looking forward to this night for weeks now. Every time she'd ever seen Caleb anywhere, he'd always greeted her politely. Always. Even if he'd been with someone else, he always made it a point to say hello to her. Tonight would undoubtedly be no exception. It was his cousin's tenth wedding anniversary, and he would be here for sure.

The evening went as planned. First came the exquisite banquet for the guests followed by the ball. Finally, a few hours later, Alice was able to take a moment and relax. She hadn't seen Caleb all evening, but she had been very busy. Even if she had seen him, it would have been impossible to say a word to him. With so much to do, so many people to attend to, "focus must be maintained," as her mother always said.

Now as Alice took a moment to rest, she poked her head out the kitchen door to see if she could find Caleb anywhere. Her position made it very difficult to see everything, so she carefully and quietly made her way further into the ballroom to get a better look. Raising herself onto her tip-toes, she finally located him. He danced with a beautiful girl with golden blond hair. Alice had often seen him with the same girl at various places, and her heart sank slightly as she realized he was probably courting the girl.

Alice watched until the song ended. Then to her horror a young man approached her from the dance floor. It wasn't Caleb, but a young man slightly older than Caleb, she guessed. Quickly, she tried to scurry away before he reached her. If her mother knew she'd been out and about, she would be doing dishes for a year. Unfortunately, the young man moved quicker than she did and suddenly grabbed her arm. "What's a fiery red-haired fairy like you doing over here?" the young man leered. Horrified, Alice tried to wriggle free of the man's grip on her arm. "I asked you a question, girl," the young man said, jerking her around to face him. He had dark hair and a nasty grin. It took every ounce of self-control she possessed to keep from screaming out and disrupting the entire evening.

Suddenly the man's grip lessened and she quickly squirmed away. When she felt she was a safe distance away, she looked over to see what had made the young man release her. Her heart gave a leap as she saw Caleb with an arm on the man's shoulder. Caleb did not look at her, but she felt a special bond with him, for he had saved her—from what, she didn't know, but gratitude towards him filled her young heart, and she loved him even more than she had before.

"What did you have to butt in for? I would've been nice," the young man said to Caleb.

"Why don't you find another girl to place your attentions on, George," Caleb said, smiling at the man. "You can do better than a kitchen girl." With that, both the young men chuckled and walked away from her without even a backward glance.

Alice stood stunned in the shadows. Had she heard him correctly? Had he meant to say something so hurtful or had he simply been trying to deter the attention of the other man? She hoped it was the latter, but as the evening wore on, and she received no acknowledgment of her existence from him, her heart became heavy. All the times he'd said hello to her or spoken with her he had done it out of chivalry. He only viewed her as an annoyance. A duty. A burden. But why should he view her in any other way? He was the princess's only cousin, and Alice was merely a kitchen servant. He was sixteen and she was only nine.

# Five

A gentle July breeze blew just enough to cool the evening air slightly from the heat of the day. The sun had set moments before, and the stars were gradually beginning to come out to play as they danced across the deep stage of evening velvet. Caleb had recovered and returned home the morning following his accident, and Alice had not seen him or heard from him in almost a week.

Alice inhaled deeply as she sat next to Clarence Hielott on a hill near the lighthouse overlooking the sea. She loved it here. She loved to watch the waves as they crashed against the beach below and loved the salty smell in the air. The smell was usually not as prominent in most of the town as it was here. Perhaps for that reason alone she loved it; she could take pleasure in the sea and its beauties from a safe distance.

"Thank you for spending the evening with me, Miss Frank. I've had an enjoyable time," Clarence said, taking her hand in his and kissing the back of it.

"Me too." She smiled sincerely at him. She had spent time with him every evening since the night Caleb had been attacked, which served as a pleasant diversion from her feelings towards the weathered sailor. Clarence was a gentleman, and she enjoyed his attentions. In fact, she'd had little time to ponder on Caleb over the course of the past week. "Thank you for bringing me here."

He smiled at her and gently cupped her face with his large, soft hand. "Well, I think the situation demands that I do this," he said, pulling his hand away from her face and positioning himself in front of her down the hill just a ways. Then he gracefully got to one knee and pulled a small wooden box from his pocket. Alice gasped as she realized what he was about to do. "Alice Lind Frank, will you marry me?"

She shook her head in astonishment and blinked her eyes before she determined that he had actually said the words to her. "I . . . I . . ." she stammered. She could not find any words to express her thoughts, for although she cared for him deeply, she did not love him.

"I think you know I'll make you happy," he said as he removed a ring with a very large, extravagantly cut diamond from the box. "I want to spend the rest of my life with you," he said, slipping the rock onto her left hand ring finger. "I want to be your guardian and your protector, and I want you to be the one I come home to every night."

Alice's thoughts staggered through her head as she tried to grasp the reality of the situation. She had suspected long ago that Clarence would propose marriage to her, but his timing left her temporarily stunned in an unnatural silence. Looking at the stone that now adorned her hand, she shook her head in wonderment. Even in this dim light it looked as though the man in front of her had somehow captured the stars of the heavens and placed them on her hand, dazzling her for the moment. Still unable to recover her speech, she leaned forward, intent on giving Clarence a hug in gratitude for his offer. Misreading her gesture, however, Clarence embraced her with a powerful, possessive kiss.

His kiss lasted longer than she would have liked and seemed to command that she follow his lead. Momentarily she allowed herself to compare his kiss to the delicious kiss Caleb had given her a week and a half before. Caleb's kiss was also demanding but passionately warm and caused her entire body to melt against his. Alice had no doubt that Clarence kissed her with the same kind of demand but Caleb's warmth was replaced with Clarence's dominating passion. He led their kiss well but obviously wanted her to follow his lead as opposed to sharing in the ritual equally and wholly together as Caleb had done.

When Clarence finally allowed their kiss to end, he smiled proudly. "I'll take that as a yes."

Everything happened so quickly, she had little time to think anything through and simply smiled, not knowing what else to do.

As the evening continued, Clarence took Alice back to her grandparents' home and told them the news. Alice, lost in the bustle of things, missed the look of intense disappointment that crossed her pappy's face. She went through the motions of the evening, enduring the inquiries and the comments surrounding the evening and their future. Alice simply stood back as Clarence answered all the questions. He then proceeded to take her to his family's home to tell his father the good news. Again, the situation was similar to what it had been with her grandparents.

Alice didn't seem to snap out of her state of shock until the following morning as she dressed and saw the ring on her finger. She frowned. It was beautiful, but it wasn't her. Thinking back to the events of the previous evening, she wondered why she'd not had her wits about her to think more rationally and tell him she didn't want to marry him. But was that really what she wanted? Did she want to marry him or not? Most girls in her position would probably jump at the chance to marry someone as eligible and successful as Clarence Hielott. So what made her so apprehensive? Was it because a certain young man from her youth still captivated her heart? But that young man had betrayed her. He'd insulted her and then ignored her. He'd never again given her the time of day before he went off to sea and disappeared for seven years. Returning from sea, he was still the same man he was when he left. The only difference between now and then was that now his childhood sweetheart had married another man, which forced him to place his attentions on someone else. Her.

He'd chosen Alice Lind Frank to place his affections on! Only one question stood out in Alice's mind. Where did his heart truly lie? With her or with Lydia Tollwhite? Alice had seen them together often since his return and she wondered why. Lydia was married with two young children. Was Caleb still in love with her and since he legally could not place his affections on her, had turned to Alice instead? Or was he making peace with his past and truly did have feelings for Alice?

Looking again at the ring on her finger, she shrugged. At least she had no doubts as to where Clarence's true feelings were. A diamond like the one on her finger could mean only one thing. He loved her. Ultimately, that's what all women want. A man who will love her and only her. Of course Alice wanted someone to provide for her physical and emotional needs. But she decided long ago that she could do without material things as long as she had love. She would give up everything she possessed to have the kind of love her father once had for her mother, and Clarence showed that kind of love to Alice.

Confident at last that this was the road her life needed to take, she looked at herself in the looking glass with satisfaction before starting a day of intense work.

"What are you doing here?" sneered Mrs. Winters as she opened her front door an hour later to see Alice standing on the porch with a bucket of cleaning supplies sitting at her feet. "Weren't you here just a few nights ago bugging me?"

"No, ma'am," Alice replied. "It was nearly a week ago." Alice picked up her bucket and brushed past Betsy Winters, letting herself into the house.

"What do you think you're doing? I didn't invite you in!" Betsy bellowed.

"I know. But if I'd asked, you would've said no."

"So then, why don't you leave?"

"Because," Alice said as she surveyed the room. "I came to help you out for a while today."

"I don't need any help. Especially from a know-it-all whip like you!" Betsy said as she hobbled back into the house.

"Is that so? Then tell me," Alice said as she pointed to the dirty dishes littering the counter, "do you just wash a plate as you need it or do you eat with your hands?" She'd infuriated the woman, but before Betsy could say a word, Alice rescinded the remark. "I didn't mean that negatively; I only wanted to come over for a couple of hours and help straighten things up. Is that all right?"

"I suppose," the woman mumbled reluctantly. "But don't expect any praise or thanks from me," she said as she retired to a room near the back of the house and slammed the door behind her.

Alice grinned proudly. With the exception of the one remark, she had remained entirely positive during her encounter with Betsy Winters. That was a feat in and of itself. Turning, she headed to the sink intent on tackling the kitchen first. It was a difficult chore, there was no denying that, but it made Alice happy to be helping the woman. Getting on in years, Betsy obviously didn't always feel up to taking care of herself or the house. That fact manifested itself in her attire that morning. Every other time Alice had seen her, the woman had been appropriately attired, but then she only left the house every other week or so. Today, Betsy obviously had not expected to have company or to go anywhere because she still wore her nightdress, and it was late morning. Shaking her head at the disgusting dishes caked with dried food, Alice continued on with her task.

Nearly three hours later, she finally finished cleaning up the kitchen. Alice stepped back to look at the work she'd done. It looked like an entirely different room. The counters glistened, the table and floors were polished, and not a single crumb littered the room. Momentarily, Alice wondered how long it would last, but she hoped the woman would enjoy having the room clean anyway.

A second later, Betsy Winters entered the room, still dressed in her nightdress and slippers. As she entered, Alice watched her face carefully. Obviously Betsy was pleased and shocked at the work that had been accomplished, but her expression was quickly masked by her usual grumpy demeanor. "Well, I see you're not completely worthless after all," Betsy said as she turned to face Alice.

"I'm glad you like it," Alice said as she went to gather up her cleaning supplies. "Now, if you don't mind, I need to go back and help Nana but I'll drop by day after tomorrow to clean some more." With that, Alice left the house before Betsy had a chance to say no.

"How did it go with old Grouch Winters today?" Clarence asked, holding her hand as they took an evening stroll.

"How did you know about that?" Alice asked. Though not opposed to his knowing of her involvement with Mrs. Winters, her curiosity stemmed from having no recollection of telling him of her plans.

"I stopped by your grandparents' place earlier to see you, and your nana told me."

"Oh."

"So, how did it go?"

"Great!" she said energetically. "You should have seen her face when she opened the door. It was priceless! And then after she saw what I'd done? Why I thought she was going to—"

"What do you intend to gain from this?" he asked, interrupting her story.

Shaking her head to clear her mind she said, "What do you mean?"

"I mean, why do you go to so much trouble for her? No one likes her and she doesn't like anyone either. So if everyone just stayed out of her way, we'd all be happy," he explained casually. "So what's in it for you?"

Still somewhat disoriented from his interrupting her, she

endeavored to push it aside. "I want to know what makes her the way she is. What drives her to be so cruel?"

"Who cares? She's grouchy and old. Let her die in peace."

"She won't die in peace because she has none!" she shouted at him suddenly. "She's grouchy with everyone because she's angry with her lot in life. That doesn't merit an invitation for people to be so rude to her."

"Perhaps people would be nicer to her if she were nicer to them," came his rebuttal.

"Or perhaps you and everyone else in this town have it completely backward. Perhaps it is the rest of us who need to look beyond her hard exterior and see the woman on the inside. Tell me something, if I were ugly, would you still love me?"

"That's a ridiculous question."

"Is it? Tell me, Clarence. I want to know. If I had been plain and ugly, would you have followed me to my pappy's shop and asked if you could call on me sometime?"

"Of course not. But you're not plain," he said as he took a quick appraisal of her from head to foot and smiled.

"So you're no better than anyone else in this town!" she said, angrily pulling her hand away from his and marching on without him.

"Wait a minute," Clarence called as he moved to catch up with her. "What's this all about?"

"It's about the fact that you are as arrogant and self-centered as . . . as . . . everyone else I've ever met," she finished.

"Or do you mean to be lumping me into the same category as Caleb Newman?" he asked casually but with an obvious air of superiority.

"What?" she yelled.

"You compare every man you meet to him," he stated simply.

"Why would I do something like that?"

"I overheard your grandmother talking to Grace Newman one day, and friends never lie to one another. Gretchen said that you are still sore from when Caleb spurned you when you were young. She said you automatically assume that all men will do the very same thing. Well, I have news for you, Miss Frank," he said as he took hold of her upper arms.

"Let me go, you're hurting me." Alice whimpered, and he lessened his hold slightly.

"I'm not Caleb Newman, and I have never given you cause to lump me in with the likes of him," he said adamantly.

"Then why didn't you tell me the entire story of how you got your scar," she said as the hurt seeped through her voice.

Taken back by the question, he seemed to recover quickly. "Because I don't like to announce my stupidity," he said quietly. Then letting go of her completely, he said looking defeated, "I love you, and I wish that would be what mattered most to you."

"It does matter to me." Feeling sorry for him, she reached out and touched his face affectionately. "I just don't like to be left ignorant of things, and I don't like being accused falsely."

"Likewise," he mumbled.

"I think I'd like to carry on the rest of the way home alone," she said quietly. He nodded, gave her a kiss on the back of her hand, and took his leave.

Late into the night, hours after Alice had retired to bed, she heard the shouting of people from the street. Quickly, she climbed out of bed and went to her window to see what had caused the commotion. To her horror, through the darkness of the night she saw a blaze down by the beach. A fire hundreds of feet tall lit up the sky like the morning sun. Billowing black smoke loomed over the beach and was reaching towards town. Men and boys on horses and buckboards or on foot rushed down the street and towards the beach. She too was concerned and, grabbing a wrap, left her room, and ventured into the main part of the house. There she saw Henry struggling to get his boots on before he grabbed the buckets that were at his feet and rushed out the door.

"Nana," Alice said as her grandmother also entered the room in her night clothes. "What's going on?"

"I don't know, peach. I guess the only thing we really can do is sit and wait," she said as she and Alice went into the parlor.

A few minutes later, a buckboard pulled up in front of the house and there came a frantic knock on the door. Gretchen raced to answer it to find Grace and Caleb on the porch. "Mrs. Lind, do you mind if Ma stays here with you and Miss Frank? Pa and I don't want her home alone."

"Certainly," Gretchen said and she welcomed Grace into the house. Caleb nodded once and then leapt down the porch to the buckboard where his father was waiting.

"I told them I'd be fine," Grace defended herself.

"Nonsense. You're always welcome here. Besides, it will be more fun with the three of us. Would you two like to go wait on the porch?"

Alice nodded emphatically and said, "I'll go get some blankets."

A short while later the women were settled onto the porch with blankets, some lanterns and various needle work projects. The air was smoky but they were too curious for information to wait inside. "It looks like we planned the entire evening this way simply so we could have some entertainment," Grace joked. Alice laughed, warmed by Grace's friendship towards herself and especially Gretchen. "So, Alice," Grace began again. "We still haven't had our little chat."

"I know," Alice said, regretfully. "I've been so busy I haven't had a chance to make it out there yet."

"I know, darling. I probably didn't do much after I got engaged either."

Alice looked down at her lap. She still had a difficult time thinking of herself as engaged. The novelty and newness of the situation sometimes embarrassed her. True, she liked Clarence more than she cared to admit aloud to anyone, but she always felt as though she had to defend herself when anyone asked about him. She knew she shouldn't feel that way, so this time she kept quiet but the feeling to defend her position still burned within.

"I think she's still a little shell shocked from it all, Grace. After all, did you see the rock that boy put on her finger?" Gretchen asked as she looked up from her needlepoint.

"No, let me see," Grace said excitedly, reaching for Alice's hand. "That's the biggest gem I've ever seen! It's beautiful!" Then seeing the look on the girl's face, the woman stopped her appraisal of the ring. "What's the matter, darling? Don't you like the ring?"

Shaking her head, Alice looked down at her hand and said, "Oh, no. It's very beautiful. It's just that . . . it's not me."

"I know exactly how you feel," Grace said sympathetically. "You know, I was planning to marry someone else before I married Augustus."

"Really?" Alice asked, her interest piqued.

"Yes, ma'am. I was engaged to marry Phil Huntsman."

"Who's that?"

"Oh, he was a local boy who grew up here before moving away some years after I married Augustus. He was handsome, ever so dashing, and he treated me well."

"Then why didn't you marry him?" Alice wanted to know.

"Well, I guess it was because I knew I didn't love him."

"Did you know Augustus while you were engaged?"

"Nope. I just knew that even if someday I did love Phil, it would never be the knock-you-off-your-feet kind of love I'd always dreamed of. And I knew that would never be good enough."

"Why not?"

Grace hesitated momentarily and Gretchen offered, "Because something in our souls can identify what we need and what we don't need in life."

"That's right," Grace agreed. "As for me, I needed someone I loved right away who would sweep me off my feet."

"Oh," Alice said. She pondered over what the women were trying to tell her and wondered if the smoke in the air was muddling her thinking. Was she reading things into the conversation or were they really trying to tell her that Clarence Hielott was completely wrong for her? Certainly neither of them would be disappointed if she decided to turn her attentions to Caleb, but she didn't know if she could put herself in that position.

As the buckboard carrying Caleb, Augustus, and Henry pulled up in front of the Lind's home nearly two hours later, Caleb climbed down quickly so he would not fall asleep. The fire had started around midnight and he was sure that by the time he and his parents arrived home, he would only get two or three hours of sleep before it was time to get up for early morning chores.

He groaned at the thought of the early start. He hadn't been sleeping well lately for a number of reasons and with not much sleep this evening, he was sure to be greatly fatigued come morning. Not to mention, he would undoubtedly need to clean up before he got any rest; soot covered his body from head to toe. His companions were also quite dirty but for reasons of debt and gratitude to an old friend, Caleb was much dirtier.

Walking up the stairs to the porch, Gretchen and Grace started firing questions about the fire at him, but he heard nothing. His attention had been arrested by the red-headed beauty that lay curled up in a chair with a blanket keeping her warm and a calm peaceful expression upon her lovely face. A smile slowly made its way across his own face until he was brought back to reality when Henry slapped his back heartily. "Yep, Caleb saved the blasted thing, but only just barely."

"You're kidding? You actually went in after that poor animal?" Gretchen asked Caleb.

"Of course," Caleb said nonchalantly with a shrug of his shoulders.

"But the ship was on fire!" Grace cried.

"That poor mutt's been Anthony's dearest and truest companion since his wife died. It was the least I could do."

"So do they know what started the fire in the first place?" Grace asked.

"Nope," Augustus offered. "I would guess one of the sailors was smoking on deck and a spark hit the wood. But there was obviously enough fuel of some kind on board for quite a blaze. By the time we got there, the ship was mostly a lost cause, and we all just kept everything around it wet so nothing else caught fire."

"Looks like we've got a sleepy one here," Henry pointed out, smiling at his granddaughter.

"Yes, she fell asleep about an hour ago," Gretchen said lovingly.

"I'll carry her into the house for you," Caleb offered.

"There's no need for that, son. I can do it," Henry said.

"I'll get her," Caleb said, shaking his head. "Besides, you'd drop dead halfway there," the young man teased. Carefully, he scooped the petite girl into his capable arms and slowly made his way into the house and down the hall to her room. As he walked, he studied her face. Her beauty radiated even in her sleep. When he lifted her, she woke up enough to snuggle against his chest where she again fell into a fitful sleep. She was perfect, right up to the very last freckle on her dainty nose.

When Caleb arrived in her room, he carefully laid her on the bed before he knelt beside her to simply gaze at her. Grabbing a cloth from the night stand and wetting it slightly from the basin of water, he tenderly wiped the soot from her face. As he watched Alice, a frown robbed her face of its peaceful appearance. He reached up and tried to smooth the wrinkles away but only managed to leave a black smudge. For some reason he never wanted this girl to feel lonely or brokenhearted. She should always be happy and smiling. She should not marry Clarence Hielott. He was a snake. A serpent. Yet Caleb was uncertain he would be any better for her. After all, if she knew what lay in his past . . . "Do you think you could ever love someone as corrupted as me?" he whispered as he looked earnestly into her face, even though he knew she would not answer him. She slept soundly and he knew even before he asked the question that she could not hear him.

He looked away from her, ashamed for even thinking such a thing. "Yes," she said in a whisper. His head shot up to see if she had woken suddenly, and he had not been aware of it, but her eyes were closed. Perhaps she had only spoken in her sleep. Then again, was it possible that she did respond to the question he posed? Absurd! Ridiculous! She lay sound asleep. How could she respond to him?

Standing to leave, he bent over and placed a lingering kiss on her forehead. She smelled so sweet. He longed to take her in his arms and hold her. Love her. Lay right here on her bed beside her and never let her out of his sight. But he couldn't. She was engaged to another man and as for himself, he was a scoundrel. A thief. A liar. How could anyone overlook things like that? Taking her hand and looking at her, he whispered, "Please love me, in spite of myself."

"I will," came her quiet reply. Caleb shook his head in an attempt to grasp the reality of the situation. Was she dreaming or talking to him? "But how? I don't understand what you mean," she spoke softly again.

He knelt beside her bed once more. "I want you to love me despite my shortcomings and my past," he whispered back.

"Wait," she called out, louder this time. "Wait, don't leave me!" came her desperate reply. "How can I fight for you if you're not here?"

Caleb stood again. Now he knew she was only dreaming. Yet somehow it felt as though she were talking to him. He wanted her to fight for him. Fight for him and help him shed this guilt that plagued every minute of every day. "I wish you would fight for me," he said quietly before releasing her hand and walking to the door.

"I will," she whispered again, and he left the room, closing the door behind him.

"What were you and Alice talking about that was so interesting last night?" Grace asked her son as he helped her clear the table from breakfast the next morning. Augustus had gone back outside already to attend to more chores allowing Grace the opportunity to ask the question that had been burning holes in her brain all night long.

"She was sleeping, Ma," he said with a yawn.

"Oh, but we heard both your voices coming from her room."

"We?" Caleb asked. "You were listening?"

Grace laughed, ever so slightly embarrassed at admitting to eavesdropping. "Well, not really. We just heard your voices. Nobody actually heard anything that was being said." She looked carefully at her boy. Something was eating at him, but she didn't know what it was or how to get it out of him. Ever since he'd come home, he'd kept more to himself than ever before. It was uncharacteristic for Caleb to keep things bottled up. "So what were you two talking about?"

"Nothing. She was sleeping."

"Nothing? Then how come I heard her voice?"

"She was talking in her sleep, I think."

"What did she say?"

"She was talking to someone and said she'd fight for them but didn't know how she would if they left her." Caleb stopped clearing the dishes and looked at his mother as astonishment filled her eyes. "For a minute I honestly didn't know if she was talking to me or just talking in her sleep."

"Maybe both," Grace said before silently scolding herself. That was not what she'd intended to say.

"What do you mean by that?"

"Do you think you could run these potato peels out to the compost pile for me?" Grace couldn't tell him anything else. She had always been a lousy liar, and she didn't want to intrude on Alice. She was a sweet girl, no matter how insecure, and Grace would not mess things up for her by telling Caleb something she shouldn't.

"Ma . . ." Caleb began.

"Run along. I'm sure your pa will need your help before you go down to the shipyard." She shooed him out the door and heaved a great sigh of relief that she'd gotten off the hook. This time.

"Well, well, well." Alice looked up to see Cora and Sally Whitmer entering the shop bright and early two mornings later. "Look who's working today," Sally said in her silky voice. Sally had never liked Alice ever since Clarence started directing his attentions towards her. Sally was a year older than Alice and Cora was a year younger. They were rude, whiny, and frankly not very pleasant to be around, though they thought they owned the charm of royalty.

As propriety demanded in this kind of situation, yet against her will, Alice put on her best fake smile and said, "Good morning, ladies. Can I help you find something?"

"Certainly," Cora sneered. "Would you be able to tell us where to find Caleb Newman?"

"No."

"Are you sure? Because we heard he made a very late house call to your place two nights ago," Sally chimed sweetly as she and her sister exchanged amused yet dangerous glances.

"Yes. It's reported that he swept you into his arms and carried you into the house to have his way with you," Cora sang merrily.

"What are you going on about?" Alice asked. The fire had been two nights ago, and she couldn't understand what these two girls were talking about. She remembered little of the evening due to utter exhaustion. The events from beginning to end were somewhat of a blur; however, she did remember her dream of being held in Caleb's capable arms. He'd visited her dreams again as he had so often in the past. This time, however, she had recognized him for who he was instead of an unknown man. In the past, he had never attempted to come near her. He simply appeared, said, "Fight for me," and then disappeared again. But two nights ago, he had carried her in his arms, kissed her forehead, and said, "Fight for me." Instead of disappearing, he lingered when she'd called out for him to wait. He then did something else he'd never done before. He spoke to her again. "I wish you would fight for me." A tear spilled onto her cheek as she remembered the beautiful dream of the man she had always loved but could never have.

Bringing her back to the present, she heard the cackling of the two girls who currently stood at the front of the store. "Oh look," Sally said, laughing, "you've made her cry!"

"Then it must be true," Cora squealed.

"What's going on out here?" Henry said as he entered the main room of the store. He wore a brown apron and a fabric measuring tape hung around his neck. "Can we help you girls with something?" he asked after quickly evaluating his frazzled-looking granddaughter.

"Yes," Cora said. "Mother sent us in for some needles and thread."

"You'll have to go to the general store then. We only sell clothes. You know that," he said as he began to herd the girls out the door. "And next time, come up with a better excuse to come into my shop." He closed the door behind them and turned to face Alice. "Are you all right, peach?"

Alice nodded as she quickly wiped a tear from her cheek. "Pappy, what happened that night of the fire?"

"What do you mean?"

"Well, those girls said . . ."

"Now you heed them no mind. You hear? It's most likely not true," he scolded tenderly.

"I know," Alice said, nodding. "But they said that Caleb took me inside and . . . and . . ." she began to sob, unable to speak it.

"Come here," he said as he stretched out his arms to her. "You know that I'd never let something like that happen to you. Especially in my own home." When that did not succeed in calming her, he continued. "Caleb and Augustus dropped me off at the house when we were done at the beach and then Caleb took you to your room and laid you in bed. That's all. He was back on the porch within a few minutes."

"Really? That's all?"

"Yes. And you should put more trust in Caleb. His parents brought him up to be a good boy. He'd never do something like that."

Alice nodded and wiped her eyes as she pulled away from Henry. "Thank you, Pappy. I should get back to work now."

Henry watched his granddaughter as she went back to her place behind the counter. She was so beautiful, but lately she seemed to doubt her own worth, and it worried him. The vibrancy she once exhibited was absent in her eyes, and he prayed she would somehow find that spark in her life again.

The following afternoon, though dark rain clouds loomed in the distance, Alice started next door to Mrs. Winters' house. She had been over one other time since her first initial cleaning day but only for a short amount of time. She found she enjoyed helping the old woman whether the feeling was reciprocated or not. The other day had been much like the first. Betsy had remained in her house dress and slippers with her hair unkempt and her house a royal mess. After Alice had tidied up the kitchen once more, she'd moved on to the parlor, but she hadn't had time to finish.

So Alice decided she would start there today and see where that took her. Every time she went over, Betsy always holed herself up in one of the back rooms of the house, so Alice had quite a bit of time on her hands to think and speculate. She became ever more curious about the older woman and her life. No pictures adorned the walls or shelves, no books, no trinkets from places visited, just clutter. It amazed her what kinds of things she found and the places in which she found them. There were many tea pots strewn around the house and even more cups and saucers. Alice smiled to herself as she hoped her service to this woman would help brighten the ever cloudy disposition of Betsy Winters.

Halfway to her destination, Alice stopped as she heard foot steps and wondered who walked so determinedly behind her. Turning, she saw Caleb striding towards her. His hair blew in the breeze created by the pace of his stride. The muscles in his face and neck were taut with anger and aggravation. He came and stopped in front of her leaving only inches between them. "You going to see Betsy?" he demanded.

"Yes," Alice replied, taking a step back.

"You and I need to have us a little chat," he growled.

"When? Now?" When Caleb nodded, she said, "But I'm going to help Mrs. Winters."

"Then I'll come too," he said, motioning for her to lead the way.

As she again began to walk to Betsy's house, Alice became very self-conscious about walking in front of Caleb. She could feel his gaze on her as she walked but lacked the nerve to turn around and insist he quit staring at her. Finally, she arrived at Betsy's house and Caleb came up beside her. She knocked on the front door. "Why . . . ? What do you want? Can't it wait until I'm done?" she questioned.

"You again?!" Betsy asked exasperatedly as she opened the door. Yet as Alice looked at the woman's face, she could almost see the delight at having company. "Who is this?" Betsy demanded as her gaze moved from Alice to Caleb.

"I'm Caleb Newman, ma'am. I'm a friend of Miss Frank," Caleb said cheerfully as he tipped his hat to the woman. Alice stood in awe. Only moments ago his appearance had held anger, but now he had a smile on his face and was just as pleasant as ever. She momentarily wondered what had caused such a sudden change in him. She allowed her gaze to follow his and she smiled. Betsy still wore her house dress, but she also wore stockings and shoes instead of slippers and her hair looked like it had been combed. Alice was suddenly hopeful that perhaps her coming to clean the woman's house had encouraged more healing than she'd originally intended.

Betsy opened the door for them and stepped out of the way. "Well, come in, I guess."

Alice smiled and said, "You're looking well today, Mrs. Winters."

"Oh, hogwash!" the woman replied.

"It's true," Caleb agreed. "I'd say you're looking mighty well and chipper today, Mrs. Winters."

"I don't want to be chipper," Betsy Winters huffed. Leaving Alice and Caleb standing just inside the door, she marched down the hall to the room she always went to when Alice came over.

"Great work," Alice said sarcastically as she went into the kitchen to heat up some water.

"What?" Caleb asked innocently as he followed her.

Alice shook her head at Caleb's attempt at innocence. As she looked at the kitchen, she was amazed at how clean it was. No dishes needed to be washed. The counters were clear and the table was clean too. Alice shook her head in astonishment. That meant Betsy had actually washed her own dishes and put them away. She put some water to boil on the stove. Once it was warm she poured it into a bucket and turned to see Caleb sitting at the table watching her with a silly smile on his face.

"Since you're still here," Alice ventured as she held the bucket full of warm water out to him, "why don't you make yourself useful?" Handing him the bucket, she led the way to the parlor and set to work.

After she'd arranged all her cleaning things so she could have them a comfortable distance away from where she worked, she finally asked, "So, what do you want?"

"What do you mean?" Caleb asked as he too had begun to clean up some of the clutter.

"When you met me outside you were mad as the raging sea and said you wanted to talk with me. So, what do you want?"

"Oh, nothing. Never mind," Caleb said, brushing her question aside.

"Never mind?" She turned to look at him with a daring expression. "You insisted on coming to clean with me because you needed to chat and it couldn't wait. And now you stand there telling me it's nothing? What are you playing at?"

"Nothing. I've just cooled off and don't need to talk about it right now."

"Oh," she said, drawing out the vowel. "So what you really mean to be saying is you'd rather not talk to *me* about it."

"No, it means I don't want to talk about it at all right now," he growled.

"It means that you only wanted to talk to me because I was the first person you saw," she cried. Then looking around and remembering she stood in someone else's home, she lowered her voice but the intensity, hurt, and anger were all still there. "It means that you'd rather keep whatever it is to yourself until you've had a chance to talk it over with Lydia," she spat.

She'd hit a chord and she knew it, but that was what she had intended to do. He had invited himself to interrupt her afternoon by saying he needed to talk with her and then blatantly refused. It made her mad that he suddenly changed his mind, and in retaliation she said something she knew would make him talk. She knew where his soft spots probably were only because they were the spots that were sore with her concerning him. So she'd flung them at him and gotten the desired result.

"Lydia's married and I'm not the kind of scum to come between those kinds of vows," he grumbled.

"But you're willing to come between other vows!" she countered.

"Name one!"

"All right," Alice needed to think for only a minute before

one came to mind. "You would do anything to break off my engagement with Clarence Hielott." That was it. Anger glowed from him. She could see the fire spring into his eyes like she'd never seen it before. "I dare you to deny it."

"Sugar, everyone in your life would love for you to break it off with that snake!" Caleb said, struggling to keep his anger at bay.

"But I gave him my word that I would marry him. That's as good as any matrimonial vow."

"No it's not!" he nearly yelled. "You can still back out of it and no legal action need be taken. With marriage, it's not so simple. Besides, Lyddie's my oldest friend, and I'd never ruin her happiness."

"Yet you seem to have no problems ruining mine."

"You're not happy!" he hollered at her.

She stood there, gaping at him. "I'm not? And just how would you know?" She felt happy. She appeared happy to everyone else. Why would he say she wasn't happy?

"Look at yourself," he said, slightly more calm and taking a step towards her. "You don't smile the way you used to."

"I can't think of any other way to smile," she retorted.

"That's because you have no reason to. But it wasn't so long ago that you smiled completely differently."

"And just how would you know?"

"Because," he said, lowering his voice and taking another step forward until he stood only a foot or two away from her, "you used to smile differently at me than you do now."

"Perhaps that's because I don't feel the same towards you as I once did."

"Is that entirely true, sugar?" he said provocatively and took hold of her shoulders.

"Yes," she said quietly as she looked to the ground.

Lifting her chin he smiled and mumbled, "You're lying, sugar. Either that, or else the same feelings are there and they too have only matured with age."

"And just how would you know what my feelings for you

have ever been?" she asked as her voice rose in volume again. She tore herself from his grasp and frantically went back to work in an effort to deter the tears that had already begun to well up in her eyes. "For the past ten years I have felt nothing for you except distaste and revulsion."

"Now they say, sugar, that love and hate are very close together in matters of the heart."

"What would you know?" she yelled as she spun around. "You with your jezebels following you around at every turn. You . . . I used to think you were a kind-hearted person. The kind of person everyone wanted to be around. Well here's some news for you: I'm not going to follow you around." Caleb stood looking in her direction, yet he did not seem to see her. He appeared to be deep in thought. At that moment, she hated him even more. How could he be so insensitive and simply stand there while she spoke to him, no matter how disinteresting the conversation was to him? "Chalk one up for the little people, I suppose," she muttered disgustedly under her breath as she turned back around to finish her chores.

"What do you mean by that?"

"I mean that you don't even listen to a word I say. You probably never have. To you, I've always been an obligation. Someone unimportant and forever the sand under your feet."

"That's not it at all, and you know it."

"Do I? Then why did you tune me out just now? Were your thoughts with some other girl? Perhaps one much more interesting and beautiful than me?"

"No," he stated simply. "I was only thinking about what you said."

"And what was that?" Alice asked, testing him to see if he had indeed heard a single word she had spoken.

"You said that for the past ten years you've hated me,"

"So?"

"Well, if I'm not mistaken, I met you thirteen years ago," he said slowly. Fear quickly enveloped Alice as she closed her eyes tightly. She would be unable to resist him if he put together that she had continually built up a wall up against him only so she wouldn't get hurt again. "Am I wrong, sugar?" came his sultry voice. Alice shook her head, not trusting her voice. She felt his hand cup her face, and she opened her eyes to look at his amazingly handsome face. "What happened, Alice? Why'd you stop talking to me? I remember seeing you over the years, but each time you'd turn away as though you hadn't seen me. Why?"

Alice shook her head and stepped away from him. If he didn't already know, she certainly could not tell him. Her heart would then break for certain. That embarrassing moment in her life was one she never wished to relive. Turning from him, she attempted to return to her work once more, but her attempt proved futile when Caleb put a hand on her shoulder and ran it slowly down her arm.

"I can't do this," she whispered and ran from him. She ran through the house and out the front door, running and running until she didn't believe it was possible to run any longer, but still she ran. Finally, thinking she might die from exhaustion, shortage of breath, or the burning in her lungs and legs, she collapsed to the ground and sobbed bitter tears. Why, oh why couldn't he choose someone else to place his attentions on and leave her alone? Her heart was tender, and she could feel it breaking all over again. True, Lydia was married, but Alice had seen the way Caleb still looked at the golden haired beauty. It was the same look he'd had in his eyes all those years ago when he looked at Lydia. So why did he insist on trying to capture Alice's attention when they both knew his heart could never belong to her entirely?

Several minutes later she sat up and looked to see where she was. Gasping, she realized her feet had carried her to her most treasured retreat. There, rising out of the ground in front of her, the old lighthouse sat looking out over the ocean below. It was ominous looking yet comforting, and she loved it. Lush foliage surrounded it and lined the cliff ledge. Slowly she rose to her feet and, wiping the tears from her eyes, stumbled to the edge.

Only a moment before she took a step beyond the bushes and seemingly to the bottom of the cliffs she heard Caleb's shout.

"Alice, wait!" Looking terribly pale, he began running faster to reach her. "Don't do it! I'm sorry I upset you, just please, don't jump," he said in between pants.

Hoping to elude him, she did take the step beyond the bushes and quickly followed the narrow path to her hidden retreat. The bushes along the edge of the cliff grew so tall and tightly together they could easily conceal a full grown man, resulting in few people knowing that anything lay beyond them. But Alice knew which bushes hid the strange, narrow path of earth that led to the secluded alcove in the cliff overlooking the ocean in all its glory, void of any bushes or other distractions. When she finally made it to her safe haven, she sat down and gazed out at the horizon. She loved to sit and observe the activities going on below. She could see the Hielott shipyard from here and the fish market along with a good share of the beach and its many visitors.

"There you are," Caleb said as he leaned down to peer into the opening. With enough room for the both of them, he plopped himself beside her and let out a long, labored breath but smiled as he looked over at her. "So, do you come here often?"

"I haven't been here in years," came her honest reply.

"I had no idea this place existed. I thought after those bushes there was nothing."

"Well, that's how it is beyond most of those bushes. You just have to know which ones to choose," she said, smiling smugly before returning her gaze to the scene before them.

After a few long minutes, Caleb broke the silence. "Listen, Alice. I'm sorry I upset you, but I have to know. And please," he pleaded with her as he reached for her hand. "Please don't run out on me again. Why did you quit talking to me?"

She looked at him curiously. Innocence plagued his eyes. "Are you truly ignorant as to the reason?"

"Yes," he said quietly, his expression only deepening in sadness.

"It was because you . . . That night," Alice began quietly and uncertainly. "At the ball when that man . . . you . . ."

"I saved your hide," he said, obviously confused as to why she would mention that long ago night.

"Well, I heard what you said to him. When you thought I'd left." She looked at him, trying to find understanding hidden in his eyes. But all she found was deepening confusion. "You said . . ." She swallowed back the tears and looked down at her hand that he still held in between both of his.

"What," he softly encouraged.

"You said that he could do better than . . . than . . ." Her voice caught in her throat. Her heart began to burn with pain, and she fought valiantly to keep her emotions in check but she was losing the battle. Fear and hurt were overruling her pride and she broke down into bitter sobbing and quickly buried her face in her tiny hands.

". . . a kitchen girl," he finished quietly with horrified remembrance before pulling the sobbing girl into his arms. "Oh, Alice. I'm so sorry," he muttered into her hair as he held her tightly. Alice allowed herself to cry the tears that had been pent up in her heart for so long. She breathed in his scent as he sat there holding her trembling form. He smelled of wind and the sea. She wanted to cry forever so he would keep her tightly in his arms, but her tears soon ran out. When she finally began to calm down, he held her far enough away from him so he could look into her eyes. "I never meant to hurt you. I only wanted to deter him so nothing would happen to you."

"So . . . you really didn't look down on me?"

"No," he whispered emphatically. "You were my dearest little friend. Every time I saw you, it brought a smile to my face. I never would've dreamed of hurting you intentionally."

She smiled, allowing herself to absorb his words briefly. Yet as she gazed into his eyes, a thought that had often resided in her mind plagued her now. "Why did you go out to sea?" she asked much to his surprise. She had told him her secret, and she remained convinced that there was more to his going to sea than he constantly let on.

The look on his face quickly turned to weariness as he said, "I'd always dreamed of it."

"Yes, but why else?"

"I don't know what you mean," he said as his eyes narrowed slightly.

"Well, everyone thought for sure you'd stay and marry Lydia. Or at least marry her before you left. But you didn't, and I want to know why. If you really loved her, why did you leave?"

"I left because I was. . . . I thought . . . because I had always wanted to," he finished harshly moving her out of his arms. "Besides, why does it matter now?"

"There was another reason, wasn't there," she encouraged.

He looked out to the ocean before bowing his head and whispering, "Yes."

"Did you ever tell anyone?"

"No."

"Will you tell me now?"

"No," he said quietly.

"Why not?" she pleaded just as quietly, as she leaned forward to look at him until she was merely inches from his face.

He looked up slowly and their noses almost touched. Her heart quickened as he gazed into her eyes and moved one of his hands up her arm and over her shoulder. "It doesn't matter now," he whispered as his gaze dropped to her lips briefly. She wanted to press the matter further but found herself mesmerized by the magic that seemed to have enveloped them suddenly. His thumb began to caress her neck as his other hand moved to her back and began to pull her onto his lap. "Can I kiss you?" he whispered as he moistened his lips with his tongue.

Her mouth began to water as she longed for him to do just that. She longed for the feel of his lips against her own. Then, within seconds of nodding her head in the affirmative fashion, his head descended and his lips captured hers in a tangle of ecstasy. He wove his magic about her, and she simply drowned in the lushness of it all. His arms wrapped tightly around her and she allowed her arms to go around his neck. She ran her fingers through his hair and their exchange deepened while the passion heightened. At that very moment, all thoughts of another woman in his life, of his snubbing her at the ball all those years ago, or even thoughts of Clarence Hielott were obliterated. For at this moment, she knew that Caleb's heart belonged to her and that hers would always and forever belong to him.

He pulled away from her for a moment and gazed into her eyes. "Give me another chance?" he whispered.

"To what?"

"To prove myself to you," he mumbled. "As your . . . friend," he finished awkwardly.

She looked deeply into his eyes. She wanted so badly to be much more than his friend, but she also needed to start somewhere with him. Then again, didn't kissing him already promote her to a higher status than that of a friend? As she looked into his beautiful eyes, she could see that he had not originally intended to ask for her friendship. No. Like so many other things, for whatever reasons he had, he seemed to be holding something back. But why? To protect her? To protect him? Or because he was scared of waking up one day to find that he had drowned with everyone else that fateful day?

Unable to speak, she nodded her head, vowing to be his friend and pulling his face forward to meet hers again as she administered a kiss of her own to him. Her longing for him felt unreasonable but he was unlike anything she had ever desired before. She could not get enough of him and her kiss seemed to portray her longing for him. When she pulled away from the kiss that had revealed more of her feelings than she'd intended, she saw an all-knowing grin spread across his face. "It's all right, sugar," he said provocatively as he began to kiss her cheek. "I like kissing you too." His kisses began to travel across her nose to her other cheek. "In fact," he whispered next to her ear. "Longing for a taste of you and your chocolate freckles keeps me up some nights." She gasped and pushed him away. He only chuckled and she realized he was merely teasing her. Then he let his lips hover over hers for a moment. "I do wish you'd call off your engagement," he said, growing more solemn.

"Why?" she whispered, nearly fainting from his teasing lips, still hovering slightly over hers. She could feel them as she spoke and it made her crazy for want of his kiss. At this moment she would move mountains for him if she could. Caleb was everything to her. He always had been. In fact, the only reason she'd settled for Clarence Hielott was because, though she'd waited for Caleb to return from sea and had never given up hope that he was really alive, he had been gone so long that she had feared Clarence was her only option. Now, as Caleb held her in his arms, gracing her with such intimate affections, she gained a little hope that perhaps he could one day be hers. Still, she needed to hear him say that she was more to him than a passing amusement.

"I'd hate to think of you kissing anyone else the way you kiss me," he mumbled and kissed her lightly.

"I never have," she said as she closed her eyes, waiting for his kiss. When he didn't kiss her immediately, she opened her eyes and saw a smile spread across his face.

"You don't know how happy I am to hear that, sugar," he said, leaning down to begin kissing her again.

# Seven

Alice pulled away from Caleb instantly with a startled scream as she heard the loud clap of thunder. They had not been locked in each others arms for long when she'd heard it. Then almost instantly the rain came down in sheets. Panic engulfed her entire being. She couldn't possibly stay here during a storm. She had to get home to Nana and Pappy. They'd be worried sick and this place was not safe. Carefully she tried to stand but had to duck her head, for the opening in the cliff had a low ceiling.

"Hey there, sugar. Where're you going?" Caleb asked as he clasped her skirts in his hand prohibiting her from leaving.

"I have to go now!" she yelled as the panic gripped her tighter. Her chest began to constrict, and breathing became more difficult. Her vision blurred, and her reason was quickly fleeing. She had to leave before something dreadful happened!

"Sugar, we're not going anywhere in this stuff. We'll have to wait it out," Caleb said as he put his hand out to feel the intensity of the rain.

"But . . . Nana . . . Nana will be worried," Alice stammered as she began to swat Caleb's hand away from her skirts.

"Don't worry. After I left Betsy's house, I saw Gretchen working in her flowers, and I told her I was coming after you. It'll be okay."

"But I can't stay here! I can't!" Panic started to engulf Alice's body and mind, and she tried to venture out into the rain again before she felt one of Caleb's strong arms wrap around her waist and pull her back to the safety of the alcove.

"What're you trying to do? Get yourself killed?" he hollered at her, raising his voice to be heard over the loudness of the storm.

"Let me go! I can't stay here!" Alice screamed as she began to kick and squirm frantically, trying to get away from him. She was, however, unsuccessful as he managed to pull her down to the ground and roll his body on top of hers so she could not get away.

"Now, I can see you seem to have some issues with storms," he said while trying to settle her down. "But it's simply not safe out there. So until you calm down, I'm just going to make myself comfy."

"Get off, you big brute! I can't breathe!"

"I'm not going anywhere until you promise me that you're not going to run out in this stuff again," he said very seriously.

Alice tried to calm down. She tried to slow down her breathing, and her racing heart but she just couldn't. Her body would simply not obey. Images of a similar storm flashed through her mind, and she started kicking and hitting her fists against the giant man that now lay on top of her. "I have to get home! I can't stay here!" she cried over and over again. Then, when it became evident he did not plan to let her up, she simply began to sob and let her hands fall away from him in utter defeat. "Please," she whispered as her head lobbed from side to side. "Please don't make me stay here! I can't bear it!"

"Shhh," Caleb said, gently caressing her face with his hand. Looking into her face, he knew something terrible had happened to her that made her deathly afraid to be exposed to the elements and away from her family. He could see the panic and fear in her eyes. Those were the same feelings he felt every time he was at sea during a storm. Ever since that dreadful night. The night he'd seen so many of his friends die. The night he'd come out a survivor and everyone else went to meet their maker. Guilt flooded him instantly. He knew of this girl's pain but he also knew she would be safer staying where she was. "Shhh," he said again as he continued to soothe her, running his fingers along her face in a comforting fashion. It seemed to be helping as he saw and felt her body gradually begin to relax. Then ever so cautiously and carefully, he slid his body off from on top of hers but kept a protective arm around her middle.

Alice felt his body leave hers and considered running but as she calmed down, she realized that going out into the storm could prove to be fatal. So she remained motionless on the ground next to Caleb. She also discovered that upon his removing himself from her, he had taken the heat he had provided for her and almost instantly she began to shiver from being wet.

"Are you cold?" Caleb asked. Alice could only nod as her teeth started to chatter. "Well, come here," he said. Scooping her into his arms, he sat her on his lap and wrapped his arms around her. "Is that better?"

"Mm-hmm," Alice said as she laid her head on his shoulder with her nose nuzzled against his neck trying to ignore the rain, which kept her a prisoner with this fabulous man.

"Good. Did you know it was a storm just like this one that sank the Blue Sparrow?" Caleb asked quietly.

Alice brought her head erect instantly. He never talked much of his time at sea, and she had certainly never heard him talk of that night in question; the one he somehow managed to live through. She gazed into his eyes and saw the deep sadness and guilt. She wanted to take it away from him. She wanted him to be happy and love her. "Please don't look like that," she whispered.

"I can't help it," he responded. "I think of what happened and I feel this incredible . . . guilt."

"But why?"

"Because I couldn't save them," he responded simply, though he wasn't looking at her.

"How did it happen?" Alice had been starving for the information for the past six years. She had longed to know why the ship went down and why it had taken with it the ever so strong and handsome Caleb Newman. When he came back, he had been so distant somehow and when the topic came up, she didn't feel it was her place to push the issue. But now that he had opened up and initiated the conversation, she planned to take advantage of the situation.

"I don't know really," he started. "The day was much like today. Sunny and clear with only a cloud here and there. The evening went without incident and then suddenly, the storm was upon us. It was like one minute it wasn't there and the next minute it was. I'd never seen anything like it before. We tried to make it to the safety boats when it was obvious the entire ship would soon go down but a giant wave came and drowned the whole ship before anyone knew what hit them." Caleb scratched his head and shook it before continuing. "Most of the crew were in their under things because it was pretty late. I'd been on watch, so I was one of the few entirely dressed."

He glanced at Alice, who sat looking at him in utter shock. He chuckled a moment before his gaze was drawn to the ocean again and he continued. "My ankle got tied up in a rope and it nearly pulled me to the bottom of the ocean, but I got it off, and when I surfaced, I tied my hand to a beam to keep myself afloat. I tried to get to some of the other men, but a wave hit me and knocked me unconscious."

When Alice finally found her voice, she said, "How did you survive for the next six years?"

Instantly, Caleb's face turned to stone. "I got on with another crew and sailed with them for a while."

"Why do you do that?" Alice asked as she moved her hands to his brown leathered face and tried to smooth the wrinkles on it.

"Do what?" he asked looking back at her with confusion now dominating his handsome features.

"Hide."

"Hide from what?"

"Everything," she stated simply. "Me, your parents. Everyone you know."

"I don't think I know what you mean."

"When I asked you how you survived, you turned all your emotions off and went stone cold in appearance. Don't you think it would make life easier for you if you were to tell someone what really happened?"

"That is what really happened," he growled.

"I know. But perhaps telling someone the entire story might make things easier to bear."

"Nothing would do that, sugar," he mumbled. "You have no idea what kind of price I wear on my head even as we speak."

Alice waited for him to expound on what he had said but it was obvious he did not plan to. Set in his ways, not even she could penetrate his walls of resistance. But she understood, for she too often put up her own walls, except he seemed to be able to puncture her walls, making it difficult to resist him.

Glancing nervously out at the elements, she shuddered. She had almost forgotten her fear of the storm while Caleb told of his adventures. Forcing her attention away from the weather once again, she turned back to Caleb and asked, "Will you tell me the real reason you went off to sea?"

"I told you already," he grumbled as he looked out into the storm.

"No, you told me what you told everyone else." Taking her tiny hands, one on each side of his face, she turned his head until he looked directly into her eyes. "I want to know why you left," she whispered.

He stared at her for a long moment until she was certain she meant nothing to him, for if she did, he would tell her. Wouldn't he? She would tell him anything he asked, if he only asked. Obviously that was the difference between them. Then the memory came of earlier when he'd asked her to give him another chance. If he wanted another chance to be her friend, didn't he need to learn to confide in her? "I want to know something from you first, sugar."

"And what's that?"

"That night, the one after the fire, after I put you in your bed

I heard you talking in your sleep. Well, I'll make you a deal with you. If you tell me about your dream that night, I'll tell you why I left for sea."

Mouth gaping and eyes bulging, Alice sat speechless. She knew which dream he referred to. It was the night he had visited her in her dreams. A thought came to her suddenly. Had her dream that night held more reality to it than she'd known? Had he really spoken to her and she to him? And how could she possibly tell him that for the last thirteen years she'd dreamt of him? Yet if she didn't, how would she ever know why he had really left for sea? Or did she really want to know?

She thought about his proposal longer than she should have and before she had a chance to say anything, he asked, "Why do you become so panicked during a storm?"

She barely heard him as another clap of thunder rang through the air and she jumped. "The dream begins with a man walking towards me out of nowhere really," she began. She would much rather speak of her dreams than her fright of thunder storms. "It used to be a man whose face was somewhat obscured by a mist. But now his face has become much clearer." She paused, contemplating the strangeness of her dream. It still made little sense, but maybe telling Caleb would help. "He stops a couple feet away. I always ask him what he wants and all he has ever said, until just recently, is 'Fight for me.' Then he is simply gone," she finished quietly.

"Do you have this dream often?"

"Not as often as I used to."

"What happens in that dream now?" he asked.

"He comes to me, lifts me into his arms, and then kisses my forehead before telling me the same thing. Then he sets me down and walks into the nothingness unless I tell him to wait."

"Then what does he do?"

"He says, 'I wish you would fight for me.'" She looked to Caleb who sat looking like he'd seen a ghost. The color had completely left his ever so tanned skin and he looked as though he might get sick at any moment. "Are you all right?" she asked.

He merely looked at her and said, "Why does he ask you to fight for him?"

"I don't know."

"And how long have you been having these dreams?"

"Probably about . . ."

"Thirteen years?" he supplied for her as their eyes locked.

"Yes," she whispered.

"Am I the man in your dream?"

"Yes," she breathed, barely audible.

Alice would have been utterly humiliated at having shared her dream with him, but she soon found herself in his tight embrace and had little time to think about it. "Why didn't you ever tell me about this?"

"What do you mean?" she asked as she pushed away from him slightly.

"Why haven't you ever told me you have that dream about me?"

"What good would it do? I don't even know what it means. Until you came home again, I didn't even know it was you. Not to mention, it's utterly humiliating discussing it with you," she said, looking away from his tantalizing eyes.

"Please," he whispered into her hair as he pulled her body against his once more. "Don't ever keep anything like that from me again."

"Why not?" she whispered, loving the way it felt to be so close to him.

He held her away from him, and his eyes searched hers. "Do you realize I talked of the sea my entire life but was always too afraid to actually go?"

"What?" she asked, completely thrown off by his remark. She could remember when she was younger, her nana would tell her about how Grace prayed Caleb would never actually go to sea. "So why did you go?" she asked when she got her bearings back.

"Because I was convinced that a girl I was waiting for to grow up would never love me unless I did something truly heroic, like go to sea."

"Why would you think something like that? Did this girl tell you as much?" Alice couldn't imagine who could not love Caleb Newman. He was so handsome, charming, and courageous. He was perfect. Who would stoop so low as to only love him if he were a hero?

"No, but she hadn't spoken to me or given me the time of day for over three years," Caleb said softly with a sense of pleading in his voice.

Alice's mouth dropped open as realization dawned on her. Could he possibly be talking about her? Was the reason he left all those years ago because she thought he regarded their friendship as an obligation? "But what about Lydia?"

"Oh, yes," he said chuckling. "We had been friends all our lives and I was interested in her, but only because I couldn't have . . ."

"Don't say it," Alice said as she covered his mouth with her hand. "I don't think I can believe it."

He pushed her hand away and said, "Because I didn't think you would ever have me."

There. He had said it and now everything was out in the air. He told her he'd left because of her, and he'd learned that she had quit talking to him because of him. The entire thing seemed to be a giant misunderstanding, and Alice felt a little dizzy from it all.

"All this time . . ." she whispered. "If I'd only known . . ."

"But you didn't know until now and now things are already complicated. I spent all those years at sea and you . . ."

"I'm engaged to Clarence Hielott," she finished for him quietly. A forced laugh suddenly escaped her lips and she shook her head. "It always seems to be something, doesn't it?" The thunder sounded but she didn't hear it as she looked at him with longing in her eyes; she was not the least bit surprised when Caleb leaned in for another kiss. However, this kiss was different than before. Before his kisses held longing and passion that seemed to be kept in check but just barely. This time his kiss held longing and passion but the years of sadness were so great, they overwhelmed the kiss making it feel nearly empty and almost final.

When he pulled away she quickly looked away from him. Embarrassed slightly, she felt somehow responsible for everything that had happened to him. "Where do we go from here?" she whispered as she played with a string that had come loose on her skirts.

Caleb lifted her chin and turned it towards him but did not speak until she allowed her eyes to meet his. "Alice," he whispered. "I don't want things to change between us. I don't blame you for my decisions or for what happened while I was gone." She looked away again, and he quickly brought her face back around to meet his. "I still want you to give me another chance. Let me be to you what I couldn't before. Let me be your friend and your companion."

"But what about Clare . . ."

"I don't give a rat's . . ." stopping himself, he reconsidered his thoughts. "I don't give a toot about Clarence Hielott. You do whatever you want where he's concerned, except marry him." Alice giggled at his protectiveness towards her. "I just want to spend time with you and get to know you again. As a friend."

"I'd like that." Alice smiled at him.

"Me too," he said, grinning. "Now, what do you want to do until this rain stops?" he said with an eyebrow quirked in mischief. Her gaze fell to his mouth, which immediately turned into a grin. "Oh, you too? Okay." Then he gathered her into his arms again and locked her lips with his. Soon he had once again woven a spell of enchantment around them both until she was in a state of utter ecstasy.

# Eight

When the rain finally stopped, the spell between Caleb and Alice was broken. Both knew they would be missed if they were to linger after the storm, yet something had changed between them and neither one could deny it. They had not only decided to give their friendship another go, they had also shared deep secrets that one only shares when in secluded circumstances. This knowledge made Alice slightly nervous. Caleb had opened up to her, and they had shared some wonderful moments, yet she knew more had transpired in the last seven years that she did not know. As he smiled at her, she decided to be patient. Perhaps in time their friendship would continue to grow, and he would tell her the rest. Then again, perhaps it wouldn't, and she would end up marrying Clarence instead. No, she determined immediately. She would never be able to settle for Clarence Hielott now. Not with the knowledge she held of what it felt like to truly be in love. She was not in love with Clarence, nor could she ever be in love with him—not the kind of love she knew she needed to have in her life. So she would wait and see what came of this new relationship and take it from there.

"We should probably get you home, sugar," Caleb whispered protectively as he looked at her with unquenchable longing.

Alice could not find her voice and simply nodded as he took her hand and led her out of the opening in the cliff, up the narrow, muddied path and out from behind the bushes into the open where the old lighthouse sat sturdy and strong on its post on the small hill. They continued to hold hands as they walked at a casual pace down the road until they came to the corner. When he dropped her hand from his, Alice looked at him curiously. They had just spent the last couple of hours together in arguments, secrets, and passion. Why would he dismiss that so suddenly? Was he not as interested in her as he'd claimed?

"Alice." He looked at her with a face that said, *don't give me that look.* "How is it going to look if we go into town holding hands? You're supposed to be engaged! Remember? I don't want to whoop on anybody today," he said, sounding a little defeated.

Nothing more was spoken between them as they continued on their way. However, rather than walk through town, they went along the back road where they would encounter fewer curious gazes. Finally, they rounded the last corner that would take them to the Lind's home. Alice could see her nana in the flower garden picking weeds again. The rain had softened the earth making the weeding easier, though it also made the job much dirtier. As Alice and Caleb approached the house, Gretchen looked up and smiled.

"Where did you find her, Caleb?" Gretchen asked.

"Out past the lighthouse," came his reply. He winked at Alice.

Gretchen turned pale and said, "Whatever were you doing out there when you knew a storm was a coming?"

Alice looked down guiltily. She knew her nana would reprimand her and justifiably so. "I didn't know the storm was coming Nana or I would never have gone," Alice said quietly.

Caleb looked from the woman to the girl as if trying to decide what the secret about that alcove was but at last he shrugged his shoulders and shook his head. "Well, at least you're both safe," Gretchen said. "Peach, why don't you run along and get your things from Betsy's and then come in, and we'll all get some supper."

Alice turned without even saying a good-bye to Caleb. Being

reprimanded in front of him embarrassed her, even though she had expected it to be much worse. The alcove was a foolish place to be, especially during a storm. After all, the ground could slide down the cliff in the rain. Someone could easily get hurt. Someone could easily . . . "Caleb, why don't you join me in the house," Alice heard Gretchen tell him.

"Oh, no thank you, ma'am. I should really be getting home myself."

"Nonsense. Your mother stopped by earlier and she and your father are joining us for supper as well."

Caleb only chuckled and followed her into the house. Alice watched him as he left. He was so fantastic to look at even as he walked away from her. He nearly always rolled his sleeves up while he worked, so his muscles were easily accessible for anyone who wanted the visual indulgence. She smiled as she caught a glimpse of his profile. His slightly rounded face made his features appear soft, giving him a boyish charm she found incredibly alluring. A furious blush rose to her cheeks when he suddenly turned and caught her appraising him. He threw her a wink and a smile but never missed a step. She quickly turned to hide her discomfort and thrill at his flirtatious gesture and made her way to Betsy Winters' home to collect her cleaning supplies.

"What do you want now?" the woman greeted harshly after Alice knocked.

"I came to get my things and to apologize for not getting much done today."

"Hmph." Betsy held the door open for Alice to enter her house.

Alice made her way to the parlor where she knew she'd left her things. Going to retrieve them, she stopped as she noticed a small painting sitting to the side of one of her dusting rags. Almost positive it had not been there earlier, she picked it up to examine it more closely. The beautiful painting portrayed a woman in her early twenties and a young boy and girl who appeared to be close in age. Alice studied the painting intently and ultimately decided the woman looked as though she might be related to Betsy. They both had the same high cheek bones and the same sad eyes but this woman had beautiful, dark hair and sat elegantly poised, while Betsy was frumpy, to say the least, with snow white hair and a sour expression.

"Pretty sad, isn't it?"

Alice turned suddenly to see Betsy standing in the doorway of the parlor. Not realizing the woman had followed her into the room, Alice wondered momentarily if the painting had been placed there intentionally for her benefit. "I'm sorry," Alice finally said. "What's sad?"

"That picture," Betsy said.

Again Alice looked at the picture. She knew people rarely smiled for paintings, but their eyes often spoke volumes. The children's eyes looked happy as all children's should, but the eyes of the woman greatly disturbed Alice. Her heart bled for the girl in the painting with those two children. "Why is this beautiful woman so sad?" Alice asked quietly, looking up to Betsy for the answer.

"Heartbreak," came Betsy's reply.

Alice could see it now: the pain and anguish of losing a loved one. A child perhaps? No. A lover. A friend. A confidant. But why had this unseen person gone? Disease? An accident? Money? What could possibly take anyone away from the beauty personified in both the woman and children in the painting?

"You need to grab hold of that boy now, or he'll never stick around." Betsy's voice cut through her thoughts.

Looking again to the woman before her, Alice was stunned at the pain that seemed to accompany her words. Fully dressed now, even though she hadn't been earlier in the afternoon, Betsy moved awkwardly to sit in a chair next to the girl and reached out to take the painting. As she looked at it, Alice saw the tears brimming in Betsy's eyes and suddenly felt the woman's heartbreak. At that moment, Alice knew Betsy was the woman in the painting and those were her children. The mystery still remained as to what had caused the pain and suffering of this old woman's heart, but Alice felt compassion for her. She was grateful she had reached out to her when everyone else ignored her completely.

"Tell me what happened," Alice said quietly, as though she might break whatever spell had caused this woman to share this secret with her.

"Not tonight. It's been a long day. But next time you come over, we'll have us a talk. And in the meantime, you hold onto that boy for all you're worth, you hear?" Betsy had spoken in a scolding tone, yet it was a quiet, loving, motherly tone. It touched Alice's heart for she had never heard the woman speak this way before.

"But what about my engagement to Clarence Hielott?" she ventured.

"Don't you know a skunk when you smell him?" Betsy asked with a little more contempt in her voice.

"So what should I—"

"I don't care!" Betsy exclaimed impatiently. "Just don't let that blond one—the one who makes your eyes glow—don't let him get away."

As Caleb sat in a kitchen chair watching Gretchen flit here and there finishing the preparations for the meal, his thoughts drifted back to the beginning of the storm. It seemed so long ago, but as he sat in thought his mind kept sticking on a particular aspect of his afternoon with Alice. She had been panicked. She had been so terrified of the storm, he could do very little to settle her down or convince her to stay put until she was calmed, which had been a challenge in and of itself. He wondered what had terrified her so. Was it the thunder or lightning? The rain? Or something else entirely? Then when they arrived at her grandparents' home, Gretchen had calmly yet ever so sternly reprimanded her for being there at all, especially during a storm.

"Mrs. Lind, can I ask you something?" Caleb ventured.

"Sure, honey. What's on your mind?"

"Well . . ." He paused, not sure how to address the subject. "When Alice left Betsy's house, I found her at that alcove in the cliffs. That is a beautiful place! I'd never seen anything like it before."

"Yes, it is very beautiful," Gretchen agreed, although she seemed to sense there was more he wanted to ask her.

"When the storm started. . . . Well, quite honestly, I've never seen anyone quite so scared of a storm before."

"That's probably true. Alice doesn't like storms at all. Even if she's home she hides under the blankets in her bed with her hands over her ears and her eyes tightly shut."

"But she's . . ."

"A grown woman. I know," Gretchen said with a sad smile and a sigh. "She's been slightly better in recent years, but not much."

"Why?" It completely baffled Caleb why such a confident woman would turn to such childish behavior at something as simple as a storm.

Before Gretchen answered, she moved over to where Caleb sat at the table. She looked at him apologetically, as though she wished she could fix Alice's anxieties because they carried with them a lot of pain. Taking a deep breath and slowly letting it out, she finally began the tale. "Some years back, there was a little girl about seven, playing around that lighthouse out there when the rain started. She went to find shelter in the alcove on the cliff but part of the edge gave way and she nearly went the fast way down the cliffs."

"I heard about that. I think I was only about fourteen or so."

"That sounds about right. This girl's daddy told her that if she wasn't more careful, one day she'd find herself in a spot she couldn't get out of. But she was a spontaneous girl and loved adventure. One day, nearly six months later, she talked her daddy into renting a boat and going fishing. Well, he didn't know anything about fishing, so he took his father-in-law along with them. Mind you, the one knew about as much as the other."

"That could be frightening. But if they were only going fishing . . ."

"Now let me finish," Gretchen interrupted. "They'd been out two hours and had even caught some fish when they saw a storm rolling their way and decided to head back in. Well, sometimes those storms can roll in pretty quick and needless to say, they were caught in the middle of it, though they were only a hundred yards or so from shore. Suddenly, a giant wave hit them and knocked the little girl out of the boat."

Caleb watched Gretchen in horror as the tragedy of the story unfolded. Flashing through his mind, he suddenly saw sailors sprinkled across the ocean but had little time to think about it before Gretchen rushed on with the story.

"The way it goes, the father jumped in after her while the father-in-law followed along in the boat. The father reached the girl and carried her back to the boat and quickly handed the girl to her grandfather. He then held tightly to the boat as another giant wave crashed down on them. The grandfather still held the girl and when they could see again, the boat was nearly filled with water. The grandfather set the girl down and began to bail the water only to notice that the father was gone and nowhere in sight. Knowing it would be impossible to find him in such conditions and that they could just as easily die if he didn't get the water out of the boat soon, he continued to bail. It was only a short time later that a bigger boat reached them and rescued the girl and her grandfather, but the body of the father was never found."

Caleb sat there stunned for a moment. What a terrible thing to have happen to a child. It must have left a profound effect on the girl, not to mention her family and friends. "I think I vaguely remember that story. Was the girl a friend of Alice's?"

"No," Gretchen whispered. "The little girl was Alice."

The entire picture came into focus for Caleb. This story explained more about the girl than just her fright of storms. It also cleared up the reason for her eagerness to engage herself in projects while pushing people away before they got too close. He hadn't realized it before, but it was something she did. When they were younger, though they never spent more than a day together at a time, she took to him like wild fire to a dry corn field. At first. But after about a year, she kept things to herself, instead of opening up her heart to people. Perhaps for that reason she'd hooked up with old scar face. He was safe. She felt no emotional attachment to him. Then again, if that were true, why did she agree to marry him? Did she feel obligated after they'd courted so long?

Then there was the issue of him. Since he'd been back, Caleb had watched Alice battle with many emotions. Only now did he realize the full extent of those emotions. For years she had dreamt of him. Maybe even loved him. Then he had disappeared for seven years just as her father had done, except he had returned. Over the past weeks, he had watched her struggle as she both wanted to be near him yet forced herself to stay emotionally detached for fear of losing someone else she loved. And now that Caleb had shared with her his true intentions for leaving for the sea, how would that factor into all of this? Would she accept him and allow herself to finally open up to him as she had once before, or would she continue to keep her feelings buried?

"I know it seems a little silly for her to be so afraid of storms," Gretchen broke into his thoughts, "but it was pretty traumatic for her. She was in shock for several months."

"I never knew . . ."

"Your mother told me she didn't think she could bear to tell you. Especially since you were so fond of your little friend."

"She was a cutie," Caleb mused with a chuckle. "She always wore those two little pig-tails that curled up so nice and bounced every time she walked. And she still has those freckles that dance across her nose."

Gretchen giggled as she too pictured the small girl in short skirts and pig-tails. The girl still possessed her childhood charm, but she had grown into an elegant woman. Caleb had noticed it the first time he'd seen her after his return. Long, copper curls hung from her head and danced with the sunlight reflecting in her amber eyes. And those freckles. They ignited something deep within him. They not only added character to her beautifully flawless face but they were sensuous, and he found his mouth watering for a taste of their chocolate flavor.

"She was a beautiful little girl," Gretchen said.

"She's still beautiful. She's just a bit taller now," Caleb said. He looked to the door that had opened ever so quietly to reveal the object of their conversation. He saw the obvious dismay blatantly etched on Alice's face at being the topic of discussion and he quickly stood. "How long until supper, Mrs. Lind?"

"Oh, probably a half hour or so."

"Good. Alice and I are going for a walk. My legs are still cramped from sitting in that alcove for so long."

"Don't be long," Gretchen said with a smile. "I expect your folks in a quarter hour."

With a subtle wink at Gretchen, Caleb walked over to Alice and held out his arm to escort her as she looked at him in confusion. "Miss Frank, I would be honored if you'd join me," he said as properly as possible, trying hard to keep a straight face. She conceded and linked her arm with his and he led her out the door.

# Nine

"Why were you and Nana talking about me?" Alice asked once they started down the road a little ways.

"Does it bother you?" Caleb asked casually.

"No, I just want to know what you were talking about. That's all."

"She was telling me about why you're so afraid of storms," Caleb said, watching her carefully.

"Oh," Alice said with little facial expression.

"I'm very sorry for your loss."

"Thank you."

"Learning your story really helped to clear up why your attitude towards me changed after that first year we met."

"You could tell . . . ? I mean, it did?"

"Yes, but not enough for me to have asked you about it. I thought it was just because you were growing up."

"I was."

"But you had to grow up all at once and much faster than most kids have to."

Alice nodded in agreement as they continued to walk side by side down the road. A hard part of her past, she still struggled with it at times and would never dream of telling the story to anyone. Fortunately, most people knew and avoided the conversation. She never told Caleb for fear that he would . . . Honestly she didn't know. Deep down she knew he never would have teased her about it or brought it up regularly to torment her. So why had she never told him before? She could not find an answer to the question, but having him know now helped to heal a part of her soul that had been damaged from that time in her life.

"So I guess a moonlit cruise on the water is out of the question?" Caleb said teasingly.

Alice laughed. "Probably." Silence followed her comment for several minutes until they turned around and headed back to the house. "How much do you know about Betsy Winters?" Alice finally asked.

"Not much. Why?" he asked, raising an eyebrow in surprise and interest.

"Just curious. She showed me a painting of her when she was very young with her two children," she continued.

"Yeah, Katie and Paul."

"You know them?"

"Not really. Ma used to know Katie pretty well until she married and moved away."

They walked in silence for a minute before she spoke again. "Why does everyone seem to think I made the worst mistake of my life in accepting Clarence's proposal?"

"Who thinks that?" he asked looking over at her. When she gave him a *don't play stupid* look, he said with a grin, "Besides me."

"Well, tonight, Mrs. Winters called him a skunk and chastised me for not holding onto you." Caleb nodded with a restrained smile. He agreed with the old woman but didn't know what to say that would not sound conceited. "What's so terribly wrong with him?" Alice asked.

"I don't know. I just don't like him." They were coming back to the house and he led her up the stairs where they sat on two rockers that decorated the porch. "Do you?"

"Do I what?"

"Do you like him?"

"Of course. I wouldn't be engaged to him if I didn't."

"Do you love him?" He looked intently at Alice. She looked down at her hands folded delicately on her lap and fiddled with the diamond that adorned her finger. She knew she didn't love Clarence, but she was unable to look at Caleb and admit it to him. So she continued to look at her hands and twist the ring. "Does he make you laugh?" he persisted. Still she did not answer. She had not laughed with Clarence in such a long time. "Does he make your mouth water for his kiss?" Again, she didn't answer. The truth was she only kissed Clarence because she knew she should—because Clarence expected it. "That there should answer your question, sugar. I think you should love the someone you promise to spend your life with. You should be able to laugh and cry together. You should long to be with him every minute he's away from you. And you should be best friends and confidants. But then that's me. Everyone's different I suppose."

Alice slowly brought her head up and forced her eyes to look into his. Slowly, carefully, and quietly she began to speak. "I do want what you speak of, but I don't think it exists for me."

"And why not?" he asked as he folded his arms across his chest and his entire face puckered into a frown.

Alice could see that her statement offended and aggravated him, but he managed to keep his anger at bay. "I just don't think it does. It's never happened to me before."

"Yes, it has," he breathed through clenched teeth.

"What do you mean?"

"Correct me if I'm wrong," he began with as much patience and understanding as he could muster in that moment. "But a long time ago you were more than willing to give your heart to me, except I was too old and you thought I didn't like you. Right?" Alice nodded reluctantly and he continued. "Sugar, since I've been home, you've changed. You act different. A little more carefree like when you were younger. I know because Ma's mentioned it." Alice blushed slightly and looked down at her lap once more. Caleb reached over and lifted her chin. "I'll do my best to make your dreams come true, sugar, but you have to give me time and give me the chance. And if you marry Clarence . . .

well, if you do, that chance won't be there."

Alice knew what he said was true but she dreaded breaking off her engagement to Clarence. She enjoyed his company, yet knew she would never love him. She also wanted everything Caleb offered but felt obligated to attempt to make things work with Clarence, even though she didn't love him. The idea haunted her for the remainder of the evening. She heard little of the conversation going on around her at supper. There was laughter, but she was unaware of its cause and often didn't laugh. Everyone dismissed it as her continuing anxiety from the storm; everyone except Caleb. Alice knew he understood the reason for her silence and felt grateful he kept it to himself.

However, his sincere concern over her situation plunged her deeper into her confusion. She knew from experience that Clarence would not be concerned for her. No. He would tell her how he felt and expect her to agree with him. Granted, Caleb probably felt that way as well but the difference was, she knew Caleb would stand behind whatever decision she made, whether it coincided with his plans or not.

Alice stood on the porch waiting for Betsy Winters to answer the door four days later. After standing there nearly five minutes, she finally heard the woman coming to the door. When Betsy answered, she looked tired and pale. Seeing Alice, she opened the door before turning and sluggishly walking down the hall without so much as a hello. Halfway to the room Alice assumed was her bedroom, the woman spoke at last. "I don't feel well and am going back to bed. Don't make too much noise."

Alice quickly and quietly set to work, doing her best to respect the old woman's wishes. She finished cleaning the parlor and put some broth on the stove. As she waited for it to warm, she meandered down the hall to find another room to clean. Rather than attend to any of the rooms she knew Betsy spent little time in, her attention was drawn to the closed door where Betsy usually hid when Alice came by.

Slowly she pushed the door open, hoping it wouldn't creak with the motion. The door opened soundlessly and she quickly looked to either side, assuring herself that Betsy was not about. Then, ever so carefully, she pushed the door open the rest of the way. Alice gasped as she entered a very large room. It was bigger than she had guessed and contained two large windows. On the walls hung numerous paintings of the ocean, the beach, the meadows, flowers, bees, and trees. They were the most beautiful things Alice had ever seen. The soft colors in some contrasted with the bold colors in others. Each told its own story. She particularly liked one that hung alone on the far wall. It depicted a lighthouse standing strong in a terrible storm. The waves, high and fierce, tossed a ship to and fro. Yet a beam of light from the lighthouse remained constant and strong.

Looking around some more, Alice noticed an immense number of paintings in stacks on the floor, lining the walls. She assumed they were blank, but her curiosity was piqued. She started to thumb through them, amazed to discover they were all painted. There had to be over a hundred paintings in this room, yet the room was tidy, not cluttered.

Turning, Alice's eye caught a portion of the room she had missed before. A small archway led out of the room into another. Curious as a cat, she made her way into the small room. The windows extended from the floor to the ceiling on two of its four walls. In the center sat an easel and a chair. Surrounding them were paints, brushes, cups, towels, and a mug of old tea. Slowly, Alice moved to stand in front of the painting. Thus far she had only seen beautiful landscapes or things one might find in nature. But this picture was different. This picture was probably the most wonderful of them all. This painting was identical to the painting of Betsy and her children that Alice had seen just the other day except for one thing. Behind the woman and two children stood a very handsome man.

A cough startled her and she quickly turned around. "What

are you doing in here? These rooms don't need cleaning," Betsy grumbled.

"I see that," Alice said, looking around at her surroundings again in awed reverence.

"Off with you now," the woman mumbled, but Alice hesitated to leave this stunning treasure she had discovered. "What do you want? Speak!" the older woman demanded hoarsely.

"I'm sorry. I just had no idea you painted. These are beautiful."

"Hogwash. They're lousy," the woman croaked followed by a deep cough that shook her entire body.

"Let me help you back to bed, Mrs. Winters," Alice said taking the woman's arm and leading her to her bedroom. Once Betsy was comfortably situated on her bed, Alice said, "I hope you don't mind my asking, but why do you think your paintings are so lousy?"

Betsy grumbled for a moment before she responded. "Everything else in my life is lousy, why shouldn't my paintings be too?"

"I think they're extraordinary! Why haven't you ever sold any of them?" Alice asked, appalled that the woman would claim such art to be no more than trash.

"I did. A long time ago," the woman said bitterly.

"Why'd you stop?"

"Why are you asking me all these questions?" Betsy demanded.

"I'm sorry. I only wanted . . ."

"I know. I know. You're just as curious as everyone else in this town. Why is old Betsy a recluse?" Betsy coughed a couple more times before she continued. "Well, I quit selling them because my feelings were hurt one day. I know that's a poor excuse, but it's true."

"Will you tell me what happened?"

The old woman glowered at her as she took the liberty of sitting on the edge of the bed. "I don't want to, but I can see there's no getting around you if you want something." Alice nodded and could almost see a smile on the older woman's face. Sighing heavily, the woman began. "I used to take paintings to the gallery in town once a month. I sold tons of paintings there, and the customers were always happy with them. The gallery even sold my paintings to some bigger galleries in other areas. One day I took in a painting, and I saw a customer there looking at one of my paintings being displayed. Well, she didn't like it and was saying all sorts of mean things about it. She was going on and on like there was no tomorrow. It just happened to be one of my favorites—one I thought was one of my best."

"So what did you do?" Alice asked, trying not to sound too intrigued by the tale but hypnotized by it all the same.

"I took the painting I was planning to drop off and left, never to return again," Betsy said with a shrug of her shoulder.

"That's terrible! Why was the customer so cruel in her appraisal if you were standing right there?" Alice was stunned. Such behavior was simply not acceptable.

"I always paint under a pseudo name," the woman said as though it were the most obvious thing in the world.

"What name is that?"

"You nosy brat! I can't be telling you all my secrets, now can I?" Betsy acted perturbed by Alice's intrusion into her now not-so-secret life, but Alice detected a smile trying desperately to creep across the woman's tired face.

"If you don't, then you'll only take all your secrets to the grave. Don't you want to pass on your wisdom? Or are you too selfish and insist on keeping it all to yourself?" Alice answered defiantly.

"If you knew how untrue that statement was young lady, you'd run away with your tail between your legs like a wounded dog!"

"Well, how can I if you don't tell me?"

"Fine!" the woman spat. "You know, I used to give my paintings away as gifts." As she spoke, her tone softened. "I was famous, but no one ever knew it was me. That was the best part. I could make people's day by giving them a Summerlee Wynter original and they would never know it only cost me for the supplies. I loved that," Betsy said with a sigh.

"You are Summerlee Wynter?"

"Yes," the woman said somberly.

"I've seen your work before. You are amazing. I had no idea!"

"Most people don't."

Alice sat in awe. She loved the Summerlee Wynter paintings she had seen, though they were scarce and hard to find. The few she had seen were her very favorites. She couldn't believe Summerlee Wynter, the famous painter, and Betsy Winters, the sour old woman from next door, were synonymous. "What other secrets do you harbor?" Alice asked then.

"What do you mean?"

"Like the fact that you're Summerlee Wynter. Do you have any other great secrets you're hiding from the world?"

The older woman laughed. The first laugh Alice had ever heard escape the woman's lips. "How you do go on!" Then, sobering, she continued. "I'm afraid that's it. Other than that my life has been pretty miserable and boring."

"Tell me," Alice pressed. "You promised you would."

"When?" the woman asked confused.

"The day you showed me that picture," Alice offered. "Please, Mrs. Winters. Tell me about your life and your heartbreak and your children."

The woman closed her eyes and took in a deep breath. She held it for nearly half a minute before she let it out. Then slowly she opened her eyes and allowed them to finally land on Alice. "I was only eighteen when I married Angus Winters, who was nearly ten years my senior. He was a handsome man, charming and well-off, but I did not love him."

"Then why did you marry him?" Alice blurted out.

Betsy glared at her and Alice mumbled an apology before the woman went on. "It was an arranged marriage, and I married Angus so as not to disgrace my name or that of either of our families. See, I originated from a very wealthy family, but the man I loved did not. Neal Moore was poor, handsome, full of life and adventure, and willing to do anything for me. When I agreed to marry Angus, it devastated Neal. We would still meet in secret, but that didn't change the agreement I'd made."

"What happened?" Alice asked after Betsy paused in her story to reflect back on her youth.

"Would you quit interrupting?"

"I'm sorry. But your story's so intriguing and you keep pausing. I am just trying to help you along."

"I get along fine, thank you! Now go get me some water before I finish."

Alice flew down the hall to fetch a glass of water. The story was intriguing in its scandalous nature, and she thrived on the fact that she had gotten old Betsy Winters to open up to her. She carefully made her way back to the bedroom with the water and handed it to Betsy. "Thank you," Betsy said as she took the glass and slowly took a drink. Alice could almost hear the time tick away on the clock beside her as Betsy slowly drank the water. Finally, the woman finished and set the cup on the nightstand near the bed.

Taking in a deep breath of air and letting it back out again, Betsy continued. "The morning I was to be married, Neal signed up as a sailor. He told me that if he couldn't marry me, he didn't want to stick around and watch while someone else did. So he kissed me good-bye and left that morning."

"So did you marry Angus?" Alice asked.

"Yes, I did. Out of duty and honor."

"But you didn't love him."

"And he didn't love me."

"That must've been awful. How did you get through your days?"

"I painted mostly. Angus was a proud man and wouldn't let me sell my work because he didn't think it proper for a woman to make any money. So I painted under a pseudonym and told him I recycled the canvases and painted over each painting. With the money I made from my paintings, I could buy more canvases.

Angus never knew, and I had enough money left over to save for a rainy day."

"How long did you have to live like that?"

"Two years. We didn't have children because we never shared the same bed. I didn't love him, and he didn't love me, and we were both aware of those facts. So we simply lived around each other and that was it."

"But those children in the picture; they are yours aren't they?"

"Yes, but they do not belong to Angus."

"Neal," Alice breathed, the realization of the immoral secret dawning upon her.

"Yes, Neal. He came home one weekend and Angus was away on business, as he often was on weekends. Neal and I spent the weekend together, and then he left again. I found out I was pregnant shortly after that and didn't know how I would explain it to Angus. Fortunately for me, I guess, he approached me and told me he was leaving."

"Where was he going?"

"He was leaving me for another woman."

"Did he love her?"

"I don't know and don't really care. So he left and that was the last I ever saw of him. Lucky for me, I had already made a name for myself and I did quite well. I continued to paint, tended to my unborn child, and waited patiently for Neal to return. It wasn't until Katie was about a year old that Neal finally came home again. He was only here for a week before he had to leave again. He loved little Katie and hated to leave, but he was under obligation. He said he would be gone another year and then he promised to come back and marry me."

"He was only back for one week?"

"Yes, and that was sufficient time for me to become pregnant with Paul. But Neal never met him."

"How come?"

"After Neal had been at sea for about three months, I got word that his ship went down."

"In a storm?" Alice asked terrified.

"No. It just sank. It was an old ship and it just . . . sank," Betsy finished in nearly a whisper. "But unlike the blond young man you like so much, my Neal never came back." Alice watched as tears began to flow down the woman's tired and wrinkled face. This woman had suffered so much; it was no wonder she was so sour to most of the world. Alice could feel her own eyes beginning to fill with moisture as she listened to the heartbreak of this old woman. "So I raised two children by myself, with no husband while enduring the ridicule and gossip the old bitties of the town dished out. When Katie and Paul were grown and had moved away, I became tired of life. Within a few years, I lost nearly all contact with my children due to their busy lives elsewhere and I simply waited for my time to die so I could be with my Neal. I have been waiting for over thirty years."

"Is that why you are so sour now?"

"Yes," Betsy whispered. "But I didn't intend to become this way. I simply quit finding happiness in life. I quit visiting my friends. I quit living my life. And now, everyone hates to be near me."

Alice sat there in silence, uncertain what to say to help ease this woman's pain. What she said was true. No one liked the person Betsy Winters had become. She was bitter, cold, and selfish—selfish in a way that was unforgivable. But today Alice had witnessed another side of the woman that most people had likely never known. This woman was scared, lost, tired, and lonely. Dealt a difficult hand, she had done a good job of coping with it despite the odds. She had made a name for herself and raised two children on her own. Most women would never dream of attempting that without a husband. But Betsy Winters had.

"Mrs. Winters, would you let me take some of your paintings into the gallery to be sold?"

"I don't think anyone would want them," Betsy said in a small voice.

"Sure they would. I've often heard talk about people wanting to find a Summerlee Wynter painting. I'm sure you could make a small fortune with all the paintings you have in the other room."

"But I don't want the money," Betsy objected. Alice marveled at the unselfish manner of the woman's comment. Obviously noticing the quizzical look on her face, Betsy continued. "I have more money than I could ever spend in the rest of my life. I don't want any more. I also don't know if I could handle listening to the critiquing of my work. It's so hard to hear someone tear apart your life on canvas."

"Then let me do it," Alice offered. "Let me take your paintings in and collect the money for you. And if you don't want the money, we could donate it to the gallery or somewhere else. What do you say?" Alice looked hopefully at the woman.

Betsy thought about it for several minutes before she responded. As Alice watched her face, Betsy's expression changed many times. Finally, she said, "I guess you could take down two or three. We'll see how that goes. But if they don't sell, we stop."

"Deal!" Alice said with a nod of her head. She was positively elated, and she could tell Betsy was excited too. Oh, the commotion and speculation this would start in town! Alice loved it and let out a squeal of delight.

"But I don't want to try for a month or two. I need to get used to the idea."

Alice nodded, still grinning furiously.

"Now, why don't you go away, so I can get me some sleep," Betsy demanded happily. She, too, was having difficulty hiding her enthusiasm at the prospect of painting for a cause again. However, Alice could tell the woman needed her sleep. Betsy had begun coughing again. Alice knew how essential sleep was to the healing process, so she rose from the bed and went to the door.

Then stopping she said, "I put some broth on the stove; would you like me to bring it in?"

"Yes, I think that would be nice. Thank you."

Alice smiled as she left Betsy's room. Perhaps the woman's heart would heal now. Perhaps she would warm up to people. And perhaps, just maybe, she would enjoy living again.

## Ten

"Thank you, Mrs. McCullam. I'll have Pappy come by after work with the wagon to pick up the bigger things," Alice said as she prepared to leave the general store the following week.

"Any time, dear. You tell your grandmother hello for me."

"I will. Thank you," she said again before closing the door behind her.

Nearly a full week had passed since her conversation with Betsy Winters, and Alice was having a difficult time keeping her newly learned information to herself. She had seen Clarence twice during the last week but only briefly. He always seemed to be so busy and, at times, he was simply too busy to be bothered with even the likes of her. Caleb had also been very busy down at the shipyard or helping his father out around the farm, and Alice felt a sadness envelope her at not having a chance to speak with him about Mrs. Winters.

Still, the beautiful morning caused Alice to smile as she walked down the street from the general store to her pappy's shop. The air held a slight chill from the previous evening, but the day promised to be warm and pleasant. Alice caught herself giggling as she watched a butterfly land on a small flower. "Good morning, Pappy," she sang cheerfully as she entered the store.

"Good morning, peach. Did you just come from Mrs. McCullam's?"

"Yes. I picked up the little things already and told her you'd be by later for the flour and such," Alice said, placing a basketful of goods on the counter.

"Thanks, peach. You're a good kid."

"Do you need any help in here today, Pappy?"

"No, thank you. I think your nana and I have things under control. You run along and have some fun," he said with a wink.

With a smile, Alice gave the man a kiss and left the store. Taking a deep breath of morning air, she headed down the street towards the docks to see if Caleb was working. She had only been down this way a handful of times since she was a little girl because it always gave her a queasy sort of feeling, but today she found she looked forward to what the end of her journey held. She started to hum softly to herself as she watched the town slowly come alive with people. It was early yet and undoubtedly within a half hour the entire town would be buzzing with activity.

"And what are you up to this morning, Miss Frank?"

Alice stopped. She knew the voice. Slowly, she turned around. "I'm off to the docks. And you?" she said politely to Clarence Hielott.

"I think I'll join you if you don't mind. I have some work to do there this morning." They began walking before he said anymore. "So were you on your way to see me?"

"No, actually. I was going to see if Mr. Newman was down there today." Alice knew this was a tender chord with Clarence, but she was tired of always needing to hide things from him. The time had come to be honest with him. She loved Caleb and had no intention of marrying Clarence. The topic had not presented itself earlier in the week and she considered herself a coward for not taking the courage to address him about it forthrightly.

Shaking his head as though he had not heard her correctly, Clarence stopped and said, "I'm sorry. Did you say you were going to see *Caleb* Newman?"

Alice stopped and faced him. "Yes, I did. Do you have a problem with that?"

Twisting his face up in confusion, Clarence shook his head

again and said, "Let me get this straight. My fiancée is going to the docks to see a man I can't stand." Alice nodded to affirm his redundant statement. "I don't think I like that. In fact, I don't like that at all."

"I'm sorry, but you asked so I told you."

"Perhaps I should make my wish clearer," he said more dangerously as he put a hand to her shoulder. "I don't want you meeting with him at all. Ever!"

"So you may associate with whomever you please, but my visitation rights are reserved for you and you alone?" she asked calmly and confidently. "I'm sorry, but I will not allow you to dictate the rest of my life for me."

"Fine," Clarence grumbled as he let his hand drop and looked away from her towards the docks. "Anyone but him."

"And why not him?" she countered.

"Because I can't stand him!" Clarence yelled as he rounded on her.

Stunned, she found she could not speak or even move. Clarence had never yelled at her. That personality trait had never been visible before. Now, more than ever before, she was grateful for the decision she had made. This was not the man for her. Someone who truly loved her would not yell at her for something as simple as going to see an old friend. Though Caleb was more than just an old friend, no one knew that beyond herself and Caleb.

Regaining her composure, Alice slowly and ever so carefully removed the ring that adorned her left ring finger and placed it in Clarence's hand. "I'm sorry," she said with little apology in her voice. "But he's my friend, and I will not have someone, especially my fiancé, telling me when I can and cannot go see a friend. So, if you will excuse me . . ." She turned abruptly and started walking down the hill towards the docks once more without finishing her sentence or waiting for his reaction.

"Wait a minute, Alice. This doesn't change anything between us," Clarence said as he dashed to her side again. "I simply don't like the way he looks at you, or you at him, for that matter. But that doesn't mean you need to be giving the ring back to me."

"Yes, it does!" Alice said angrily. Suddenly she stopped, causing him to retrace his steps back to her. "I refuse to let you dominate my every action. I want to be my own person, and I don't want to always wonder if it's something you would approve of or not. Besides, this marriage would never work out between us because I think you love me about as much as I love you."

"I do love you. Desperately!" Clarence pled in an all-too-well-rehearsed fashion.

"Don't tell me that. You would never defend my honor, were that issue to ever come up. If we were to marry, I would forever have to run everything I did past you. And furthermore, I don't love you. So if that isn't enough incentive for calling off this engagement, then I don't know what is."

She brushed past him in an effort to continue on her way, but Clarence seized her hand, halting her progression. "What would you do if I told you that Caleb Newman isn't what he appears to be?" His tone was dangerous, making her uneasy.

"I would say that you are gravely mistaken," she said with as much confidence as she could muster.

"Oh, but you would be wrong, my dear," he said in an unfamiliar, sinister voice. "If that's what you think you want, I will let you run to him. But know that when he breaks your heart, I will still be here waiting for you."

"Then you'll be waiting a very long time," Alice spat.

"Go then, Miss Frank. Go. Run into the arms of a pirate for safety from the wretched Clarence Hielott."

"What are you talking about?" Alice asked, uncertain she had heard him correctly. Had he referred to Caleb as a pirate? How could that possibly be? Caleb was not a thief. He was kind, honest, trustworthy, loving. . . . Wasn't he?

"So I see he hasn't told you either. The coward!" Clarence said with a menacing chuckle. "That's right. Your dear friend, Caleb Newman, is a pirate."

"How would you know?"

"Richard Forkworth, my most trusted friend, found out on

one of his excursions and filled me in on that little detail."

"I don't believe you," Alice said with not quite enough conviction. After all, the six years following his disappearance were still largely in question.

"Well, it's about time you started believing something, Miss Frank. And like it or not, he *is* a pirate and I can prove it. That was how he survived all those years. He's lied to you and everyone else in this God-forsaken town. He came upon a pirate ship and rather than be killed, he became a pirate. He pilfered, he plundered, and now he is more than just a little wealthy. Yet he keeps it from his poor family because he's selfish, he's a coward, and he's a rotten liar." Clarence chuckled as he continued, and Alice became all the more uncomfortable. "But if you think you would be happier with him than me, go. And I'll wait for him to break your heart."

Alice couldn't believe what she was hearing. Caleb? Her Caleb? How could he possibly engage in piracy? Even to save his own life? Wasn't he more honorable than that? Yet something in Clarence's eyes told her that what he had spoken was at least partly true. Or was it? Alice yanked her hand free of Clarence's grasp and ran towards Caleb and the docks. Surely he would clear up the story for her.

"Ouch," Caleb muttered to himself shaking his hand and putting his thumb to his mouth after he managed to smash it yet again. Everything he'd done today had needed to be redone or fixed at least twice. He couldn't get anything right. If only he could keep his thoughts on his work instead of that fiery red-headed beauty he had fallen in love with. Again.

Thinking of Alice always made him smile. She was so spunky and independent. His love for her had taken flight, just as it had so long ago. It had lain dormant for so many years but now it soared into the heavens, and he loved it.

"How's that rigging coming along, son?"

"Slowly, I'm sorry to say." Caleb chuckled as Anthony Hielott approached. Anthony was a good looking man in his own right. He was tall and lean with skin as tan as any sailor. He had light brown hair and a neatly trimmed mustache. He was a second father to Caleb, and Caleb thought the world of Anthony. Mostly he appreciated the man's willingness to hire him upon his return home.

"Yes," Anthony said, coming to stand beside Caleb and slapping him on the back. "Women'll do that to a man. How're things going between the two of you anyway?"

Caleb was not surprised by the comment. He had told Anthony of his relationship with Alice and the man had been thrilled. Though Anthony loved his son, he felt Clarence did not deserve Alice, especially because of his actions of late. Caleb liked the way he and this man he admired held few secrets from one another. "I haven't seen her in a week or so, but I think we're making progress."

"Good. I'd hate to see her actually end up marrying Clarence. Did you hear what he's been up to most recently?"

"No, what?" Caleb asked, setting down his tools and turning his full attention to the man in front of him.

Anthony looked around briefly to make sure that no one nearby was paying attention to the conversing pair. Assuring their privacy further, he lowered his voice slightly as he spoke. "Well, he doesn't know I know. Because if he did . . . well, I think things would be a mite different." The older man scratched his cheek as he twisted his face to the other side before he resumed his tale. "Well, you know that slimy Richard Forkworth?"

"Yeah. Those two were always hanging out when we were young."

"Well, he sails one of my ships now. In fact, his ship came in just two days ago. Well, last night I heard him and Clarence out by the docks, so I stuck my head out the office window to see what was going on. I saw Clarence paying Richard cash for something and then the two started hauling about a hundred barrels off the ship. I watched close and noticed they took them to the old abandoned warehouse I don't use any more. So early this morning, before anyone was up and about, I snuck over there to see what they've got in there. And I'd be a donkey's hind end if I weren't shocked out of my mind at what I saw. Why I thought I'd been slapped in the face when I discovered those barrels were full of opium."

"What're they doing with a hundred barrels of opium?"

"Well, I wondered that too. So I snooped through Clarence's desk, and do you know what I found? Of course you don't. I found official receipts for those barrels along with letters and some other stuff. Anyway, from what I gathered, Clarence's buying barrels of opium from China, illegally, and then selling them to ships to smuggle into Britain. And Richard is his go-to guy. What do you make of that?"

"Well, I have to say I wouldn't put it past him to do something the likes of that."

"No kidding! It's the devil I've raised, it is," Anthony said with a shake of his head.

"Don't say that. You did the best you could. It's not your fault he turned out the way he did. You didn't raise him to be like that. He picked that up somewhere else."

"You're right, my boy. You know, I'd always wondered how he paid for such a big rock for that ring he gave Alice." Anthony shook his head in disapproval before he slapped Caleb on the back again. "Well, at least I have you."

Caleb smiled. Anthony was a good, honest man. Clarence on the other hand was a weasel. It made Caleb mad to think about the strawberry-blond haired man. He wasn't even a man but rather a snake. How could anyone betray such a wonderful father as Anthony Hielott? "Do you think that's what started the fire awhile back?"

"Yes," the man affirmed. "That run Richard made was shorter than intended, so they must've had their supplier meet them halfway or something. But I don't know what else could have caused a blaze like that. You remember a while back, that article in the paper?"

"Yeah. Who was that who got arrested?"

"I don't know. It wasn't a local. Someone who'd just come in on one of my ships. Anyway, one of the sailors said he'd had chests with him. So we checked them out, and they had opium in them. Naturally I called the sheriff, and he took care of it without putting a bad mark on my company's name. But I think he was just a pawn in Clarence's game."

"Why don't you tell someone?"

"Clarence takes care of the books and all the legal stuff now—you know that. He undoubtedly has something in there protecting him if I were to ever find out about all this. And I can't possibly buy him out. When I signed him on as a partner all those years ago, I never dreamed something like this would happen to my company because of it. But now, it looks like I could lose everything to my demented son."

"Don't worry. It'll all work out somehow," Caleb said in an effort to console the man.

"Hey, isn't that Alice?" Anthony asked, placing a hand to his face to shade his eyes from the morning sun.

Caleb looked in the direction Anthony had indicated. Sure enough. A petite young woman was running down the hill towards the docks. However, he also noted that a man sauntered along some distance behind her. Caleb's jaw clenched tight as he put together who the man undoubtedly was. Poor Alice. What had Clarence done to her now?

Alice's mind relaxed somewhat as she approached the ship-yard and saw Caleb standing with Anthony amid the bustle of people at the docks. Huffing and puffing for air, she closed the distance between herself and the two men, only momentarily embarrassed about her out-of-breath state. Her run had not been long and it had mostly been downhill, but the entire time she had spent rehearsing in her mind everything Clarence had told her. Seeing Caleb caused the tears to start trickling down her face. He could not possibly be a pirate and if he were, his motives had to be different than Clarence implied. They just had to! Running all the faster, she ran to Caleb and Anthony, threw herself into Caleb's arms and allowed her tears to flow freely upon his cotton shirt. He simply held her as she cried her seemingly unending tears.

Eventually Caleb pushed her away slightly and looked deeply into her eyes. "I told you not to let those petticoats of yours get twisted into knots," he said with a teasing chuckle. "Now tell me," he indicated towards Clarence with a nod of his head, "how'd he upset you this time?"

"I . . . I can't believe it. It's . . . too horrid."

"You must believe what he told you at least partially. Otherwise we wouldn't be having this conversation. Now tell me, sugar, what did he tell you?"

"I told her about the last six years of your pathetic life. I was the one to expose you for what you really are," Clarence said, approaching the group. Caleb simply glared hatefully at the man.

"And what is that?" Anthony asked his son.

"A thief, a liar, a coward . . . and a pirate," Clarence said smugly.

"Why you lying devil, you! Who taught you to weave such lies?" Anthony snarled as he headed towards his son, his hands in fists ready to do bodily harm to his own flesh and blood.

"Leave him be, Anthony. He holds the cards on this deal," Caleb said stalling the older man. "What do you want Hielott?" he then asked Clarence.

"What do I want? I want the girl, of course. And I want you to be at the bottom of the ocean like you were supposed to be. But since you're not, we'll have to make do." Alice, who had been silent, took a step to the side of Caleb to keep out of Clarence's reach. "So," Clarence said taking a step forward. "You let me have Alice, and I won't tell anyone where you are."

Caleb hesitated as he thought on the man's offer. "There's only one problem with that."

"Which is?"

"I can't force the girl into your arms if she doesn't want to go. So, I guess the deal's off."

"Fine," Clarence said. "But you'd better watch your back from now on Newman. I know how to locate and contact your former ship. One wrong move and I'll let them know where to find you. And let me tell you, if they knew you were still alive, they'd be here before sunset."

"Enough with the threats, Clarence. Go get some work done before the boy finishes you off," the older man growled in an authoritative tone. Clarence glared hatefully at the man he'd always called father but obeyed him and took his leave.

Caleb sighed as he continued to hold Alice tightly against his own body. How could he have let it come this far? How could he have pulled her into this? Even though he couldn't possibly admit his feelings for her, she had always lurked in the back of his mind. Always. There was no denying that. She had always been there. That fiery hair. Those amber eyes. How could he have allowed this to happen? He should never have come home. It had been a selfish thing to do. He admitted now that she was truly the reason for his return. Not Lydia. Never Lydia. It was because of Alice he had left and the same person had spurred his desire to return. It had always been her.

And yet, here she stood—scared, lonely, and longing for a comfort he could not provide. Yet there were details Clarence had not uncovered. Caleb was sure of it. Still, he wanted to lash out at the serpent. He wanted to, and he would, but now he needed patience. Time would prove the snake a liar, a thief, and a coward. For now, Caleb would wait. He would comfort and befriend his beautiful Alice. He wanted to leave and take her somewhere safe, but she would undoubtedly be hurt or killed if they were ever caught. He could leave her here in the comforting arms of her grandparents, but he could not endure the separation. Or he could wait for fate to bring his destiny to him. So he would wait. Patiently.

Looking up into his eyes, Alice marveled at his protectiveness of her. He never once allowed Clarence to make an advance towards her. He only held her tightly and lovingly. The tears continued to stream down her face as she looked at him now. He was so handsome! So manly! So wonderful. Yet he still hid something from her. She could feel it. And for every part of her that wanted to know the truth—that wanted to know what constantly lurked in the shadows—she wasn't sure she ever wanted to know everything. All she cared about was that Caleb now held her in his very capable arms and this was where she wanted to stay.

"Why do you let him upset you so, sugar?" Caleb asked as he gently pushed a strand of hair behind her ear with one hand while the other hand still held her waist. Her hair had no doubt come loose while she had been running, and Caleb could tell she was self-conscious about her casual appearance.

"He . . . he said you were a pirate. I didn't want to believe him. But the way he said it . . ." She paused. How had he said it? What was it about the way he said it that threw her mind into a whirl of questions? Had she simply known he spoke the truth? Was that what made her so upset? She shook her head, not sure of her own thoughts.

"What? How did he say it?" Caleb questioned.

"I don't know," she said, still shaking her head as she looked up into his eyes. "I don't know what went on while you were away. I don't. I haven't pressed for the knowledge and you haven't offered it. But I just get the feeling . . ." She paused. Should she say what had popped into her head when Clarence made his revelation? She swallowed hard. "I just get the feeling that for some reason he's not too far off."

"Now you don't let that rotten son of mine give you grief about our boy Caleb. He's a good, honest man. I swear it," Anthony said, trying to console her.

Still, as the man spoke she watched Caleb's expression change from one of concern to one of defeat. His brow no longer wrinkled, but his eyes drooped downward in a frown and so did his mouth. He instantly looked nearly ten years older than his mere twenty-six years. She slowly reached up and put a dainty hand to his whiskery face. He hadn't shaved that morning, but Alice found she didn't mind. It was alluring in a rugged sort of way and she smiled, suddenly wanting to take his face in her hands and kiss his worries away. She had an unimaginable yearning to know him, to own him, to have him for her very own. She stopped her thoughts, however, when his eyes finally found hers. They had changed somehow. In a few seconds they had gone from their usual crystal clearness of the sky to a dull and dreary gray color almost as though the sky had clouded over suddenly. "Talk to me," she pleaded in a whisper, fearful that he might otherwise allow stone walls to surround his heart. "Please."

"I'm sorry, sugar. But he's right," Caleb managed, just above a whisper.

"Now you listen here, boy. I don't want you paying any heed to what Clarence says, you hear?" Anthony exclaimed.

"But, sir, it's true. I was a pirate. It's a bit different than what you must be thinking, but that doesn't change anything. It's still true," Caleb said with a bit more volume to his voice.

"How can that be?" Alice asked.

"After the Blue Sparrow went down, I managed to stay afloat due to a log tied to my wrist. I somehow made it through the night and when I woke up, I was on a pirate's ship. They allowed me to heal from my wounds simply because, for a time, I couldn't remember what happened. It was probably nearly a year later when I got my full memory back."

"So what happened after that? Did you leave?" Alice asked.

Surely once he learned who he had been, he would attempt to come home. Then again it had taken him an additional five years to return home. So what had happened?

"I couldn't leave. I had already signed a contract to stay on for five years and I still had four left. So when I came to . . . well, Captain Andress took to me like butter to bread. He treated me like a son.

"He took me aside one day and said, 'I knows you ain't no pirate.'

" 'So what are you going to do to me?' I asked.

" 'Well, since I like you so much,' he said, 'I'm gonna let you stay. But you have to promise not to tell anyone who you is. I don't want no mutiny for this.'

"So I stayed silent. Then about five days before my service was up and we were docked at a little town up the coast a ways, old Crane and Holden finally cracked the case. Me and them . . . well, we didn't ever get on too well. Anyway, they finally figured it out and threatened my life. 'Once I tell everyone who you is,' Crane said to me, 'I'm gonna have you keelhauled 'til yer dead.' "

"What does it mean to be keelhauled?" Alice asked.

"Simply put," Caleb began. "They take rope and tie your legs together and then your hands. There's a rope that goes under a ship to clean off the seaweed and critters from the under side. When a man's keelhauled, they tie him to this rope and send him headfirst into the water. Then they pull him along under the water along the bottom of the ship by the rope until he comes around to the other side. Then they send him back again."

"How awful!" Alice gasped, utterly horrified at the image of Caleb being forced under a ship while bound by rope. "So what did you do?"

"First, they beat me up pretty good. They left a nasty scar on my back that still gives me fits from time to time. But as soon as I could move again and before anyone woke up, I jumped ship. Then I wandered around for near to a year before I came back here."

"Why didn't you come back immediately?" she asked.

"And lead them here? No way. I decided it was best to lay low for a while. Never know when something foul will cross your path." It was obvious Caleb had referred to Clarence as being the "foul" one but Alice chose not to draw attention to it.

"Why don't you kids run along. You can finish up tomorrow," Anthony said with a smile to Caleb. Caleb nodded his appreciation and took Alice's hand in his to lead her down the sandy beach.

How heavenly and romantic to be walking on the beach with Caleb Newman. Actually, to be walking anywhere with him, hand in hand, was heavenly. Alice was still astonished by what she had learned from him and felt there was probably more to it than what he had said. Still, she would not push him to tell her. She was sure he would divulge the rest when he was ready. For now she would simply enjoy their time together. Smiling, she realized she had been staring at him and focused her attention in front of her instead.

Years had passed since she had been to the beach. The water terrified her and the beach lay close enough to the water to be too close. So she had stayed away. Yet there was comfort in knowing Caleb held her hand as they walked. He walked closer to the water than she did and for the first time in over ten years, she felt safe. Completely and utterly safe. She loved the feeling and wished she could bask in it always. But that was not her fate. She was sure of it. So she enjoyed the feeling while she could.

"You broke off the engagement, huh?" It was more of a statement than a question.

Alice nodded. "How did you know?"

"Why else would he threaten you with my past?" Caleb asked but did not look at her.

Eventually, Caleb led her around a corner to a secluded portion of the beach. She could no longer see the docks or ships anywhere. The cliffs overhead were so high up that she couldn't possibly see anyone at the top if they were there. They walked over to a sandy spot where Caleb sat down, rolled up the legs of his pants and removed his shoes before he said anything further to her. "Sometimes I miss it," he said, gazing across the calm, glassy surface of the water; the sun reflected brightly off its surface like a mirror before it was dashed into pieces upon the shore.

"The sea?" Alice asked.

"Yes. And the men. Most of them were poor but good men who just wanted an easy life."

Alice nodded, pondering what he said. She had always imagined pirates to be mean, smelly, and foul. Pirates raped woman, stole money, and killed people. They weren't nice! But Caleb had lived with them. He had been one of them. Was it possible that not all pirates were as immoral and heathenish as she'd always thought?

"Did you really steal things?" she asked.

"I had no choice, sugar. That's what pirates do. If I wanted to live, I had to do my share of the work. I'm not proud of what I did but it's how I survived. And before I made my way home, I tried to help out people in need as a way of making restitution for the way I had lived as a pirate."

They sat for awhile in silence. Each lost in his own thoughts. Alice could not possibly comprehend what Caleb must be thinking, so she allowed her mind to think on other things. Such as love and life. "Did you know Betsy Winters paints?" she asked suddenly.

She smiled, thrilled to have thrown Caleb off by her comment. His astonished expression still mingled with his sorrow and guilt but the surprise and interest seemed to be dominating his face as he sat there in wonder. Shaking her head, Alice giggled and said, "Oh yes! That room she locks herself in is her studio. Her paintings are truly magnificent. And the biggest secret of all . . . You'll never guess." Enjoying luring him into her story, she watched his face intently as his expression changed from a tired, sorrowful look to one of excitement.

"Come on, sugar. You have to tell me the rest," he pleaded.

"What will you do if I don't?"

"Kiss you until you can't breathe," he growled dangerously.

Alice giggled. "You rogue! I guess I had better scoot closer, so you can reach me better," she teased as she moved closer to him. He looked at her in surprise and she laughed. "All right. I'll tell you." She paused for a moment to allow her laughter to subside slightly. "She's really a famous painter. She paints under the pseudonym Summerlee Wynter. Can you believe it? She's Summerlee Wynter!" Alice exclaimed, barely able to withhold her excitement.

"Who?"

"Don't tease!" she said with a playful slap as Caleb burst into a smile. "I know you know who. She's your mother's favorite painter."

"I know. She's always wanted one of her paintings too. You don't suppose . . ."

"What are you thinking?"

"Ma's birthday's in a couple months. You don't think Betsy would let me buy a painting, do you?"

"I don't know. It's worth a shot. She told me she'd let me take some down to the art gallery to sell, but she wanted to wait a while."

"Well, you get to working on Betsy, and I'll see what I can do about Clarence and his threats."

Alice was suddenly uneasy. "What can you possibly do to thwart him?"

"Oh, I think I have a few tricks up my sleeve he doesn't know about—or won't think about," he said mischievously. "Now in the meantime, let's work on that 'kissing the breath out of you' thing."

All her anxiety left instantly and she grinned as he attempted an evil laugh. "Pathetic!" she squealed bursting into laughter.

"What?"

"I don't know how you ever lived the life of a pirate. You're just too . . . too . . ." she stammered trying to control her laughter and struggled to find the right word for his flirtatious yet silly manner.

"Well, I'm still a heathen, so you better watch out," he growled while his eyes danced with mischief.

"Oh yeah?"

"Yeah!" he countered. "Just watch how skillful I am in my seduction of you!"

Alice's laughter and mirth turned instantly to yearning as he began to tease her with his affections. He pushed her gently to the sand and covered her with his torso as he bathed her face and neck in kisses. An inextinguishable burning buried within her ignited as she allowed her hands to caress his chest and feel every well-defined muscle beneath his shirt. He was incredible. "Caleb, I . . ." she began, only to have her near confession of love stopped as his mouth descended possessively and passionately on top of her own. She longed to tell him of her love for him, but at the moment she could only relish in the fact that she was the lucky recipient of his delicious, demanding kisses.

And yet, for all the passion and desire she felt in his kiss, she felt as though she needed more. She longed to be closer to him. Longed to be a part of him. Longed to know his secrets and to love him freely. She suddenly pushed him away from her and looked deep into his eyes. Would she ever have the love she'd longed for but never believed would be hers? Now that she knew his secrets, would Caleb leave her in heartbreak? She looked deeply into his eyes for the answers. His eyes were now crystal blue. Clear of all the clouds that had tainted them before. She searched for the answers and what she found was hope. Hope that her dreams of him could exist for her. Hope that he could love her more than life itself. And hope that she could be worthy of his love.

# Eleven

The following morning, Alice dressed quickly, skipped break-fast, and was out the door before anyone could question her. The revelation she had received yesterday had kept her mind spinning much of the night. She still had many questions and concerns, but most of all, she worried how Caleb might react now that she shared the knowledge of his past. Would he feel threatened and leave again or would things continue on as they had? She needed to get to him and let him know that his past did not bother her and she simply wanted to be with him always. She hurried down the quiet streets of the town as indiscreetly as possible and reached the Newman's home in record time.

Grace answered the door and to Alice's horror, Grace told her that Caleb was not about the farm doing early morning chores as she had hoped. "Why is he going to the palace?" Alice inquired. Her worst nightmare seemed to be playing itself out. The only reason for him to go the palace would be to consult with or confess to his cousin about what he'd been up to for the last six years. And then what? Would he be thrown in prison like some criminal? Or would he be forced to hide in some remote location for the rest of his life?

"He just said he needed to talk to Lillian and Lawrence about something," Grace said, confirming Alice's fears.

Alice shook her head, trying to imagine what Caleb planned

to do. Nothing good could come from his visit to the palace. "Has he already left?"

"He went out to tell Augustus where he's bound and then I'm sure he'll be off."

"Maybe I'll go with him," she suggested. Perhaps she would be able to talk him out of seeing his cousin, and he would be free to stay here with her.

"Darling," Grace began, "tell me truly. How do you feel about all this?" Alice wasn't surprised at all by the question. After she and Caleb surfaced from the beach, he had taken her home, after which he was bound for his own home to tell his parents.

"I don't really know," Alice said truthfully. "All I do know is that Caleb is a good and honest man."

"Yes he is. Don't ever forget that, no matter what happens," Grace said with a loving smile. "Oh look, here he comes," she said pointing to her son who was rounding the side of the house.

Sure enough, Caleb had seen them and strode with angry determination towards them. "What are you up to today, sugar?" he asked gruffly.

"I . . . I'm supposed to meet my mama today at the palace, so I thought I might join you," Alice stammered, saying the first thing that came into her mind.

"Sugar, this is something I—" Caleb began with a look of defiance evident on his handsome face.

"I'm just planning to accompany you to the palace. That's all," she said curtly with a glare of her own. It upset her that he didn't want her company, but she would not let him be rid of her so easily. She didn't know what he was up to, but she wanted to find out in order to keep him safe.

"Well, I'm off," Caleb said to his mother with a kiss on her cheek. He then proceeded to leave without even a glance at Alice.

Stunned that he would ignore her so, she said a quick thank you and good-bye to Grace before running after him. "That was pretty rude."

"Rude, huh?" he growled without even looking at her. "You

show up on my doorstep, get information out of Ma, and then invite yourself along without my consent. And you think I'm rude?" He stopped abruptly and grabbed her arm, making her stop as well. "Let me ask you something, sugar. What makes you so sure I want your company?"

Stunned into silence, Alice stood gaping at him. Wasn't it only yesterday when they had basked in each other's kisses and secrets on the beach? Wasn't it yesterday when the truth had finally come out after she had broken off her engagement? So where did this anger and hostility stem from? She stood there in total disbelief. Was this the same man she had fallen in love with again? He certainly wasn't acting like the same man.

"Look," he said more humbly. "I'm sorry I dragged you into all this. But I have to make it right. And if you're with me . . . I can't get distracted. You understand? With everything coming down on me at once, I feel like I just got kicked in the head by a stubborn a . . . um, mule, and I don't want you to get hurt too," he said more tenderly and apologetically.

"I simply was going to accompany you. I had no intention of . . ." She felt the tears beginning to burn behind her eyes. He had hurt her only because he wanted to protect her. While this knowledge comforted her, her heart threatened to tear in two. It was then she understood that whatever stood between her and a future with Caleb could certainly take him and all hope of having him, away from her like a wave in the sea; yet, she would not acknowledge defeat. So, straightening her shoulders and swallowing the emotion in her throat, she confidently looked him in the eye. "I only want to help. But if you don't want my help, please know that I'm behind you as . . . as your friend," she faltered over her words before turning and stumbling up the road to the palace on her own in front of Caleb, blinded by her tears of hurt and frustration.

Caleb knew he'd hurt Alice and wanted desperately to run after her and make things right, but he couldn't, not right now. If he planned to live through the next week, he needed to stay strong and collected; and those things seemed to fly by the wayside when Alice Lind Frank was anywhere near him. He had no doubt Clarence could make true on his promise concerning the members of the Silver Snake. For that very reason he wanted Alice as far away from him as possible. There was no telling what those men might do if they knew he had any interest in her. Therefore, he watched as Alice staggered away from him and did his best to push his feelings of guilt and anxiety away from his heart.

"Hello, Lilly," Caleb said to his cousin as he was shown into a room in the palace. Placing a kiss on her cheek, he asked, "Where's Lawry?"

Lillian nodded to a servant who stood near the door. The servant then quickly and quietly left the room. "What brings you here?" she asked Caleb with a twinkle in her eye. She knew how uncomfortable being at the palace made him. It had to be something important to bring him here without invitation.

"I need some advice, and I think you or Lawry might be able to help."

"What if we can't?" she asked teasingly.

"Oh, come on, Lilly. Don't do this," Caleb whined.

"Why not? You teased me to no end when I was younger. Now I can't tease you?"

"This is serious, Lilly!" he complained. "I'm in some serious trouble, and I really need your help."

"Your highness?" the servant addressed Lillian as he reentered the room. "His highness will be with you shortly."

"Thank you," Lillian responded. "It's a good thing Lawrence likes you so much Caleb. He doesn't drop everything for just anyone."

Caleb threw his cousin a disgusted glance. She infuriated him so much sometimes. If he weren't in need of her counsel he'd . . . Well, he didn't know. But he wouldn't stand here and take her teasing. Sighing, he figured he probably deserved at least some of her teasing, since he had been such an innocent tease when he was young. Therefore, he tried to force her remarks to leave him unscathed. Caleb's parents had raised Lillian and even though she had married when he was six, he still felt a close connection to her, despite what he claimed, and did not wish to ruin that relationship.

"Oh, come on, Caleb. I'm sorry. Why don't we sit down and you can tell me about your little cherry tart," she said, leading him to some chairs and sitting with the grace befitting a princess.

"Cherry tart?" he questioned as he followed her over to some very plush chairs. He plopped down in one next to his cousin and stretched his feet out in front of him. "You know, Lilly, I think you may have hit the nail on the head this time." He chuckled and shook his head. The phrase described Alice perfectly—a cherry tart—sweet and tasty, forever making his mouth water for her kiss but with a sour streak that came up when he least expected it. "She's doing well, I guess."

"Is she still involved with Clarence Hielott?" Lillian asked with distaste evident in her voice. Obviously Grace kept Lillian well informed.

"Yes and no," came his reply.

"What does that mean?" Lillian asked leaning towards him as if she were about to hear a real juicy piece of gossip.

"Well, she broke off their engagement, but he's convinced she'll come back to him."

"Why is that?"

"Caleb!" Lawrence Phelps exclaimed as he burst through the door. "It's so good to see you. Unexpected, but good." Caleb stood promptly and the men shook hands. It had been long ago decided that Lillian's family need not bow to the royal family in such private settings. "So, to what do we owe this great honor?"

"Well I was about to get to that." Caleb took his seat again, only with a little more grace than he had done before; Lawrence followed suit. "Like I was telling Lilly here . . . well, I guess she doesn't really have much to do with it."

"Who?" Lawrence asked, obviously clueless.

"Alice Lind Frank," Lillian provided. "Apparently she broke off her engagement with Clarence, but Clarence expects her to crawl back to him."

"Why is that?" Lawrence asked.

Caleb pushed his hands through his darkening blond hair. When he'd first come home, it had been bleached white from his years in the sun but now that he was spending less time outdoors it had darkened slightly. "Well, I guess I'll have to tell the whole of it, regardless of what I want," he mumbled with agitation and impatience.

So Caleb began to tell the story as it had unfolded yesterday. He started with Alice and Clarence and led them through the hour following. He even told them of his conversation with Anthony. He then told them of his years on the Silver Snake and how he had come home. He told them everything. When he finally finished, Lawrence let out a long breath of air as though he'd been holding it for a long time while Lillian simply shook her head in disbelief and wonder.

"Do Grace and Augustus know?" Lillian asked with awed reverence.

"Yes. I told them last night."

"Only last night? Why if you were my son, I would have strung you to the nearest pole by your toes!" she exclaimed.

"I know." Caleb chuckled. "Thank goodness you're not my ma!"

Lawrence smiled as he stood, went to the window, and stared out over the countryside in deep thought. Slowly and methodically he began to rub his chin. Caleb knew he only did this when the wheels in his head were really turning, trying to come up with a solution. A substantial amount of time passed in silence and Caleb saw a flicker of mischief in Lawrence's eyes for a moment before he turned and walked back to his seat.

"So then," Lawrence said when he had taken his seat again. "I have an idea of a way to help you out of this mess, but it may be time consuming and most likely quite dangerous."

Caleb nodded solemnly though his heart held the slightest bit of anxiety. He already knew the situation was precarious and any action to be taken would undoubtedly be very dangerous.

"Caleb, this will be a great risk. Are you willing to make that sacrifice?" Lawrence asked.

"As long as it will keep those I love safe, I am willing to do anything," Caleb announced with conviction.

Lawrence nodded at Caleb with a satisfied smile before standing and walking to a desk in the corner to retrieve some ink, a quill, and parchment.

"What brings you here, peach?" Theresa Frank asked as she wiped her hands on her apron. Alice had let herself in the servants' door in the back and gone straight to the kitchen where she easily found her mother and a few other servants.

Alice smiled up at her. "Does a daughter need a reason to see her mother?"

"I guess not. But . . ."

"But nothing. I just wanted to see you. A friend of mine was coming this way, and I thought I'd keep him company," Alice said while embracing her mother in a hug.

"Him?" Theresa asked, pulling away slightly to look at her daughter. "This wouldn't happen to be the same 'him' that your nana talks about constantly, is it?" Theresa asked. "The one who came back from sea?"

Alice blushed. "Yes."

"Well, what mischief is he about today?"

Alice did her best to keep her emotions at bay as she spoke. "He wanted to talk to his cousin about something." The panic and fear she harbored on his behalf suddenly surfaced, and she burst into tears. "Oh Mama! I think he's in more trouble than he tells me! I'm scared for him! I really am. He's shut me out and I can't reach him. No good can come from this. He will be killed for sure!"

"Peach, I'm not sure what you're talking about, but I doubt he's in over his head. Men like him seldom are."

"But I fear he is this time! Clarence Hielott is trying to bring him down. And you know that when Clarence gets it in his head to—"

"Yes, I know," Theresa hissed. "You don't have to tell me about that . . . snake, that . . . cad!" she spat.

Alice sat momentarily shocked by her mother's outburst. Theresa had only ever spoken politely about Clarence before. For that matter, other than Alice's relationship with him, she was unaware that her mother even knew him. "Why are you so venomous towards him?" she asked curiously.

"I'm sorry, peach. I know you are planning to marry him," Theresa apologized as she led her daughter by the hand to a nearby table where they sat down together.

"Actually I broke it off with him only yesterday."

"Praise the Lord! There is mercy in the world!" Theresa exclaimed looking up to the ceiling and putting a hand to her chest, as though she were talking to God himself.

"What are you going on about?"

"Oh, nothing."

"No, you can't 'oh, nothing' me after a scene like that! What do you have against him?"

Theresa sighed heavily before she continued. "You remember that day your daddy died?"

"Yes," Alice said skeptically. She didn't know how that would have anything to do with Clarence but she listened patiently to her mother anyway.

"Well, I went with your daddy when he rented that boat. Back then Hielott & Son was the only place around here a person could rent a fishing boat." Theresa looked down at her hands that were wringing together on her lap. Suddenly she pushed them apart and looked up at her daughter. "Mr. Hielott was sick with a bug of some kind that day, so his son, Clarence, was holding down the fort. I didn't like him from the get-go. He had this evil little twinkle in his eye that made me uncomfortable, but what could I do? Challenge him? Anyway, he told your daddy everything he'd need to know about the boat except for one thing."

"What was that?"

"When your daddy asked him if someone could ride along who knew the area and would be willing to go with you, Clarence said that no one was available."

Theresa grew solemn and quiet. Alice knew the woman felt guilty about that day. Alice had her own guilt, but nothing could change the past. Her daddy was gone and no amount of wishing would bring him back. "When the storm came, I was terrified. I waited all day at the docks and knew your daddy wasn't back yet. I went to Clarence and yelled at him for a quarter hour to no avail. He only stood there smiling."

"Smiling? Why?"

"I don't know," Theresa sighed in defeat. "He said it wasn't his fault that you all went out during the stormy season. Then he simply sauntered away." She dabbed at the moisture which had begun to form around her eyes with the corner of her apron. "I found out later that there were three available and able-bodied men who could've gone along and perhaps prevented . . ." She gasped slightly as a sob escaped her throat. She put a hand to her mouth to prevent the emotion from gaining control of her entire body before she continued. "You know, I've always blamed Clarence for your daddy's death."

"Mama, that's terrible! You know he had nothing to do with it."

"No, but he could have given us a little more precaution or sent someone with you. Your daddy didn't know a thing about the sea. The boy was simply being lazy," Theresa finished in a whisper.

Alice put her arms around her mother in a warm hug. "Well, there's no need to worry, Mama. I'm not marrying him and he can't hurt us again."

"Don't be too sure about that, peach. You be careful, you hear?"

"I will, Mama. I will."

"How was visiting with your mama today?" Gretchen asked later that evening as she and Alice were cleaning the dishes after dinner.

"Good," Alice said carefully. "Nana, if you and Mama never liked Clarence, why'd you allow me to entertain a relationship with him?"

"You want us to dictate everything in life to you?"

"Well, no . . . I just wonder why no one ever said anything to me before now."

"Sometimes people can be wrong in judging another person's character."

"But you hated him," Alice said still very confused.

"True, but you didn't. Whether we like it or not, you have the ability to choose and make decisions for yourself. We all just prayed that someday you would see the truth, before it was too late." Gretchen smiled lovingly at her granddaughter, proud of the girl for her determination and strength. Alice had always proved to be a pillar of light to others, but as Gretchen looked at the girl now, she saw sorrow and uncertainty etched in her eyes and on her face. "What's eating at you, peach?"

"I'm just worried about Caleb," she said, making her way to the table to sit down. "Yesterday we had no secrets and today we are complete and total strangers. I just don't understand it."

"There's no need to worry, peach. He's a big boy. I'm sure he'll be able to handle himself."

"So Grace told you?" Alice asked and Gretchen nodded. "I just don't know why he would treat me like this. This is how it all started, you know."

"No, I don't know," Gretchen said as she came to sit with Alice.

"Oh."

"Tell me, peach. This is how what started?"

"Everything! He snubbed me at the ball so long ago, and I quit talking to him. Then he left for sea because he thought I didn't care; only to have his ship sink. Oh, Nana! What am I going to do if he leaves again? I don't think I could handle that!" she said, allowing the tears to flow down her cheeks.

"Don't worry. Everything will work itself out. I don't think you need to worry about Caleb leaving for sea again unless it was the only way to fix things. I think he has too much at stake this time."

"Caleb, what is it you're planning to do next?" Lydia Tollwhite asked the following morning as the two friends walked side by side down the main street of town.

"Lawry wants it to stay classified, and without his and Lilly's help I will never be free from all this."

"That's not what I mean and you know it," she said looking up at him disapprovingly.

"I don't know, Lyddie," he said, knowing full well the topic his friend was trying to address. "Sometimes I feel so lost but I don't want to hurt her again. I've done that once. She didn't deserve it then, and she doesn't deserve it now."

"I know, but you still need to tell her."

"I don't know what to tell her. I don't even know what to expect," Caleb said, shaking his head from side to side.

"I don't think you have really tried," Lydia reprimanded. "Why don't you just tell her and get it over with."

Caleb's face contorted with confusion as he looked down at the blond beside him. "What are you going on about? I already told you I don't know how. I swear, Lyddie. Sometimes you are the most exasperating person I know," he said as he stopped to look at his friend.

"You love her, don't you?"

"What?"

"You do. It's why you left the first time, too, isn't it?" Lydia asked, understanding reflecting in her eyes.

"Now come on, Lyddie." Caleb winced, looking away from Lydia.

"It is," she said with understanding. "I saw it in your eyes back then, I just didn't understand it. It was love, but not for me. Never for me. You loved her. You always did and you still do. Don't you?"

Caleb stopped and finally looked down at his beautiful friend. Her hair shone of gold while her features were as soft as silk. "How do you know so much?"

"You're my friend. I just don't want to see you make any more mistakes," she said, smiling up at him.

"Who said going to sea was a mistake?"

"I'm not sure it was. After all, if you hadn't gone I never would've found my Spencer." Caleb pulled a face and she laughed. "Oh, come on. He's not that bad."

"No, he's not. There are worse men in the world," Caleb admitted regretfully.

"Yes, there are. And if you don't step up to the plate, they may take everything you've fought so hard to obtain."

Alice stepped out of her pappy's tailor shop with a lavender dress in hand. She'd told her nana she would deliver it to Mrs. McCullam today at the general store. She walked towards the main street and stopped abruptly at the corner. There, in front of the general store, stood Caleb along side the beautiful Lydia Tollwhite. Alice watched in horror as Lydia gently touched his arm and lovingly gazed into his eyes. They exchanged a few words before he bent and kissed her cheek. Alice felt humiliated. Had she really been so naïve as to think he could see anyone beyond Lydia? All this time he had claimed that Alice was his reason for leaving, yet there he stood with Lydia, showing his affection for her in public. *What now?* Alice wondered. Now that she knew where his heart really lay, where did that leave her? She wouldn't run back to Clarence. No. She was wise to his ways now. Still, the heartbreak she felt from losing Caleb seemed more than she could handle. It was like watching her daddy drown in the ocean over and over and over again. Could she really let Caleb get away with this?

No, she decided. She would show him that she was strong. She didn't need him or anyone else to make her happy. So, straightening her shoulders and lifting her chin, she slowly and carefully crossed the street to the general store. She felt smug when Caleb recognized her as she approached and his eyes dropped with guilt. Once across the street, Alice smiled at the pair, said a pleasant, "Good morning," and entered the store, closing the door quickly behind her. A fiery blush washed over her cheeks and her heart beat so fiercely it nearly pounded itself out of her chest.

"What's the matter, dear? Is everything all right?" Mrs. McCullam asked, obviously noticing Alice's frazzled state.

"Of course," Alice lied, suddenly a little out of breath. Shaking the despair from her head she crossed the floor to the woman. "I just came by to drop off the dress you ordered for your daughter. I hope it fits," she added with a smile and placed the dress in the woman's arms.

"Thank you. I'm sure it will be wonderful. Is there anything else you need today?" the woman asked admiring the beautiful craftsmanship of the dress.

"No, thank you," Alice said kindly. Taking a deep breath, she turned and exited the shop. Once outside, she turned away from Caleb and Lydia, who were still standing in the same spot, and walked towards the meadow. Walking briskly, as though she were late for something, she did not look behind her. She didn't care if Caleb felt guilty for being caught with Lydia. She didn't care if people looked at her strangely as her pace increased. All she wanted was solace. She needed an out; an escape from life and the pains it was causing her heart. The meadow would serve nicely, for she seldom went there and she would have no memories of him plaguing her.

She was nearly out of town when she finally broke into a run and allowed the tears to stream down her face. She felt angry, betrayed, and hurt. How could he lead her to believe he had feelings for her when he still harbored feelings for another woman? A married woman. It was deceitful, and it tore at her heart in a way nothing ever had before. When she reached the meadow, she headed for the hill with three trees. Finally reaching her destination, she threw herself upon the ground and cried in anguish.

# Twelve

"Caleb," came Lydia's soft voice from somewhere. He'd seen Alice leave the general store and knew she was upset. He tried to force his feet to go after her but they remained rooted to the ground, lost in thought until he heard Lydia's voice again. "You need to go to her."

"I don't know if it would make a difference," he said in defeat. "She's obviously come to her own conclusions. Who am I to tell her differently?"

"You're probably the only one who knows how to reach her," Lydia encouraged.

"But I don't. I don't even know what I'm doing anymore. How can I help her to come home if I'm not there myself?"

"Because you love her and she deserves to hear you say it."

"I don't know how. I don't even know that she'll listen now."

"You need to try—for your own happiness and for hers."

Caleb followed Alice to the meadow, not sure what to expect. He knew what she must think, seeing him with Lydia, but confound it all! Lydia was his friend. Why shouldn't he spend time with her? He reconsidered his question as he stood back and watched Alice on the hill crying. A thought struck him. He loved her. More than words would ever be able to express. He knew Alice loved him for he saw it in her eyes every time he held her in his arms. This was the first time in his life he thought about it, however, and the realization came to him that he had only ever felt this way towards Alice Lind Frank. Perhaps that was reason enough to spend less time with Lydia. After all, she had replaced him with Spencer as friend, confidant, and lover years ago when she married. Perhaps it was time he replaced Lydia, too.

As he neared Alice, he felt the first drops of rain and glanced up at the sky, not having seen the clouds approach. Then again, his mind had been on other things. Slowly he made his way to the small hill overlooking the meadow. The area, this time of year, with all the flowers in bloom was a beautiful sight to behold. Instead of reflecting on the beauty of the meadow, however, he focused his attentions on the beauty lying before him. Her fiery hair danced madly in the breeze and could not be discouraged in the least by the rain that tried desperately to still it. As the rain fell even harder, Caleb stared at the sobbing girl. What had she done to deserve such a cruel punishment from him? Nothing. Perhaps that was what tore at him the most. She was so innocent. She had so much love to give, and he was undeserving of that love. Undeserving of her. Yet she seemed to give her love to him willingly.

He noticed his wet clothes clung to his body as the rain now came down in buckets; he again looked to the beautiful porcelain doll that lay dry and crying beneath the tree. He moved closer to her in an effort to shelter himself from the elements. Sitting on the ground he reached a hand out and placed it gently on her shoulder, causing her to jump and turn her hard, glaring eyes on him.

"Alice, I . . ." He started but couldn't seem to finish. The look in her eyes tore at his heart and ate at his soul. She sat there loathing him, and he knew he deserved nothing less.

"Don't bother wasting your breath on me," she spat. "I saw enough earlier. There's no need to pretend anymore," she cried and turned her back to him.

"But, Alice, I . . ." he began again desperately.

"Don't," she whirled around and yelled. She had stalled him with a look of hatred but as she continued, he could see the hard emotions rinse away with the rain as they were replaced with sorrow and heartache. "I know you love her and she is very beautiful. I just . . ." She stopped, battling with her emotions. "I just wish you loved me instead," she finished softly before she darted away from the protection of the tree, running down the hill and into the meadow.

Caleb watched her leave, stunned by her words. His heart ached for her as the distance between them grew, yet he could only watch her run farther and farther away. He continued to watch her until the danger became imminent. Surely she saw it too! But it quickly became evident she was blinded to the circumstances. Caleb leapt to his feet and charged after her. During their short encounter, the river had begun to rise. With the storm as intense as it was, the river would certainly overflow soon. He rushed to her as quickly as his feet would carry him, but the ground was soft and soggy, making progress slow and difficult.

He glanced up again to see which direction Alice had gone. To his horror, she was nowhere to be seen. Almost instantly the absence of thunder and lightning was relinquished by the heavens as lightening flashed through the now darkening sky with a loud clap of thunder following closely behind. Panic gripped him. Where was Alice? Suddenly he saw her near the river's edge some distance away. She struggled to stand in the almost knee deep water looking for safety. Knowing there was none nearby, Caleb set out at a dead run for her. The river was rising fast and he became frightened for the both of them.

When he looked up again, he saw that Alice had climbed onto a large boulder near the river. The boulder, nearly three feet tall, now appeared to be only a foot tall as the water continued to rise. He made his way to her the best he could, fighting valiantly against the elements of nature. By the time he reached the boulder, the water had risen to his knees. "Come on!" he hollered to Alice with his hand outstretched to her. "Let me help you!"

"Why don't you just leave me alone!" she hollered back, desperately trying to keep her balance on the slippery orb upon which she stood.

"Come on, Alice. Don't do this," Caleb began. Seconds later he watched as Alice lost her footing, slipped off the boulder, and hit her head, rendering her unconscious before she hit the water. Caleb's thoughts and memories were in a jumble, but this moment was not about thinking—it was about saving Alice from a horrific death. He lunged into the water trying desperately to grasp some part of the girl to pull her to safety. Still, he could not shake off the images that constantly plagued his mind of a similar storm six years ago. Frantically he began looking for Alice but every time he saw a log or small animal bobbing up and down, he pictured members of his crew on the Blue Sparrow that he had been unsuccessful in saving. He began to panic. Alice was nowhere to be seen. Searching more frantically, he knew he had to find her. He would surely die if he were unable to save her.

Suddenly, he saw her briefly before she dipped back under the water. Sloshing and splashing through the deep water, he made his way to her and plunged under the water several times until he was finally able to get to her. He held her close. He had saved her! Only a second later, however, it became evident that her breathing had stopped, and he nearly gave in to his panicked state. Regulating his breathing and trying to think clearly, he cradled her petite form against his body and made his way back towards the hill with the three trees. Slipping occasionally, he finally made it to his destination where he gently set her on the ground. He laid his head against her chest to listen for her heart beat and breathed better when he found one, no matter how faint. Tilting her head back, he closed her nose and breathed into her partially open mouth. He did this only twice before she began to cough and spit out water.

He looked up to the heavens in thanks. She was alive. Things could only get better. In the meantime, he knew the importance of getting her warm and dry so she could rest. Carefully he lifted her once more and started for town.

"Oh, Caleb! What have you been about this time?" Grace hollered at her son, seeing him staggering down the partially flooded road carrying a lifeless body. The rain had decreased drastically. Caleb neared the house, and Grace watched in shock as she realized the lifeless form in her son's arms was Alice Lind Frank. "Quick boy! Get her in the house!" she said to her obviously fatigued son. "Put her in Lillian's old room," she directed as Caleb entered the house. "Set her on the rug, and I'll get her out of those wet clothes."

Grace looked on in wonder as Caleb nearly collapsed next to Alice when he set her down. Quickly and carefully, Grace set to work taking off Alice's wet things. Once she succeeded in stripping the girl of her day dress, Grace realized Caleb was still in the room. "Where are your manners, boy? You run along and get dried off too." Caleb lumbered from the room and Grace finished taking off Alice's wet things and clothed her in a dry night gown. The girl had obviously suffered from shock among other things, so Grace quickly got her into bed. When Alice lay resting peacefully, Grace finally made her way into the kitchen where she saw Caleb nibbling on a biscuit.

"What happened?" she asked.

"We got stuck in a storm," he said casually.

"Don't play smart with me. I could've guessed as much. I want to know how the two of you found yourselves in such a predicament," she said in a scolding tone.

"Ah, come on, Ma. What does it matter?"

"Oh, but it does matter, young man," Grace stated defiantly. "If I'm going to be caring for the girl, I have a right to know what happened to her. If for no other reason than her grandparents need to know."

"All right. She fell off a boulder and hit her head. Then it took me a while before I could find her under the water."

"She went underwater!" Grace squealed.

"Ma, please! Do you want me to finish?"

Grace nodded and Caleb proceeded. "When I found her she wasn't breathing, so I blew into her mouth like I saw a guy do at sea when a man fell overboard and quit breathing."

"Well, it obviously worked. But I still don't understand why you two—"

"That's the whole of it Ma. Now, I'm beat. I'm going to go lie down for a bit," Caleb said as he left her to her thoughts.

Grace would admit to being naïve at times, but she certainly knew her son was withholding information from her, though she guessed it had little to do with getting stuck in the storm. Something had happened today that had distressed her son greatly. She had her ideas, but knew Caleb would not offer the information freely. At least not without a fight. So, she decided to keep her mind busy and went to the kitchen to make a cake.

The hour was late. Everything was dark, but squinting hard, Alice saw a figure in the doorway. It was him, though she was uncertain if he were real or merely a product of her state of delirium. Surely she would know when he approached her, but he remained in the shadows. Alice closed her eyes and tried to sit but her body refused to obey. Her arms and legs were as heavy as logs and hurt like crazy to boot. Her head felt as though it had been struck by an anvil and her throat burned with fire. It was an effort to breathe. Each breath felt like it would surely be her last.

She opened her eyes again—only slits for they would open no further—to find him still standing in the doorway. She wanted to yell at him. To despise him. To hate him. But she was mute and her heart ached with love for him. Blinking to rewet her dry eyes, she watched as he finally, slowly approached. He looked tired but handsome all the same. He walked towards her, just as he always had in her dreams, and she tried to smile, but the muscles in her face would not respond. Then he did something he'd never done before. He sat next to her and pushed one of his hardworking, calloused hands gently through her hair. A smile crept to his face, not the joyful smile she longed for him to share with her, rather a smile of finality.

"I'm sorry this happened, sugar," the blurry Caleb whispered in her dream as a tear leaked from his eye.

*"Please don't cry,"* she tried to soothe but to no avail. Her words were as nonexistent as the movements in her limbs. Still, she felt he heard her plea when he chuckled and wiped embarrassedly at his tears.

"It's a good thing you're asleep or you'd think me a baby." He chuckled.

*"No. Never,"* came her heartfelt reply.

"Alice, I came tonight to tell you good-bye."

*"What?"*

"I know if you were awake you'd never let me go, and that, among other reasons, is why I need to leave tonight," he said, still brushing his fingers through her hair. "I can't tell you everything and I don't even know if I'll make it back. But if I don't, ask Lilly to tell you. She loves you as much as everyone else in my family does. So she'll tell you."

Alice lay there motionless, not only from her paralyzed condition but from what she was hearing. *Surely you are just a dream,* she said to herself. He would never go back to sea. He couldn't! He had too much at stake if something were to happen. Didn't he? She had seen him with Lydia only earlier that day. Was it possible that since he could not have Lydia, he felt nothing else mattered?

"Sugar, I want you to know . . ." he paused and cupped her face. "I've always loved you. And if I don't return . . . know that I'll always be thinking of you."

He placed a light kiss on her pale, still lips and headed towards the open door. *Wait! Please wait!* she called to him. *Don't leave me! I love you.* Yet no matter how loud her heart cried out to him, he continued to move away from her. Nearly in despair, she tried one last time. "Wait!" she managed to choke out in a faint whisper.

He stopped and turned. Another one of his sad smiles spread across his face. "Fight for me, sugar," he whispered to her from the doorway. "Fight for love." Then he turned and left through the open door.

# Thirteen

The brightness in the room, even with the drapes pulled, made Alice squint through her closed eyelids as she awakened. She remembered her dream of Caleb vividly and told herself over and over that it was precisely that—a dream. Yet as she lay in bed, she dreaded entering back into reality. As long as she slept, the evening with Caleb had been a dream. If she opened her eyes, something inside her said it would be much more devastating than that.

As she gradually became more aware of things, she heard the whispering of voices across the room. They were female voices and Alice suspected one belonged to her nana. She rolled her head to its side and was amazed at the ease with which she accomplished the task, but it was accompanied by intense pounding. Ever so cautiously, she opened her eyes to discover it was evening and the bright light was due to the fire from the other room and a few candles that adorned the room where she lay. The room was slightly musty but clean and feminine, though it did not belong to her. She suddenly realized she was not lying in her bed nor was this her nana's house. Frightened slightly, she sat up abruptly as though she had been lying on hot coals, only to collapse back onto the bed, overcome by dizziness and a painful throbbing in her head. As she fell back to the bed, she hit her head on the head-board causing even more splitting pain. She gasped and reached up to grab her injured head, noting how easily her arms obeyed her mind's simple command. The noise caused the whispering to stop and brought both Grace and Gretchen to Alice's side.

"Oh, thank the Lord you're all right!" Grace whispered.

"How are you feeling, peach?" Gretchen asked, gazing expectantly at her granddaughter.

Rubbing at the new bump on her head, Alice answered, "Fine, I think. At least I'll survive, but at the rate I'm going, I don't know if my head will." The women laughed softly but Alice caught the nervous glances the older women threw each other. She knew something was amiss and also knew exactly what it was before either woman said a word. Caleb was gone. He'd gone to sea and he might never return.

"When did he leave?" Alice asked to the surprise of the other women.

Gretchen looked to Grace and nodded her support. Grace's eyes filled with tears as she began to tell Alice what had transpired. "Caleb brought you here from the meadow two days ago," Grace began.

"Two days ago? I've been asleep for two days?" Alice gasped.

"Yes, peach, and we've been so worried," Gretchen said. She gracefully knelt by the bed and began running her fingers through Alice's tangled hair.

"The next morning he was gone," Grace said with a sob. "He left a note explaining that he needed to leave and if anything were to happen to him, only then would Lillian be permitted to tell us all the details." Grace wrapped her arms around her middle and hugged herself as she sank onto the bed. Rocking back and forth, the tears streamed down her tired face.

So many questions raced in Alice's mind. Where had he gone? What was the urgency? What purpose would his leaving serve? And why was Lillian the only one permitted to know anything? However, Alice remained silent. This must be very difficult for Grace. Caleb, her only son whom she'd already lost once, might never return. The woman was doing remarkably well under the circumstances. So rather than bombard her with unanswerable questions, Alice lay there quietly, waiting for Grace to unload her emotions.

While Alice waited, she watched Grace. She somehow looked older than she had the last time Alice saw her. Her hair had turned to dull gray from its normal shade of silver and was pulled into a loose bun that was falling from its place at the crown of her head. Her eyes had bags under them, and her face had red splotches scattered on her cheeks from crying. Her countenance held a look of defeat, and Alice knew that when she had discovered Caleb was gone, a part of the wonderful, spunky woman must have died. Caleb was her life and, this evening, that was very evident.

"I don't know what I'll do if he doesn't come home," Grace finally whispered.

Alice felt her energy fading quickly. Her dream of Caleb quickly faded to a horrific reality of his absence. She wished her health was better so she could somehow bring him home safely, but that was not possible. As she lay there, she could feel Grace's pain coupled with her own broken heart wanting the only man she'd ever loved. Ever so suddenly she felt herself drift back into unconsciousness.

Nearly two weeks later, the bell in the store rang, letting Alice know someone had entered while she worked in the back room doing some filing for her pappy. It had taken her nearly a full two weeks after her disaster in the meadow to finally feel well enough to help out in the store again. Together with the fact that no one had heard anything from Caleb, her enthusiasm for life had reached a dangerous low. Henry was grateful for the help because he and Gretchen were scheduled to go visit Mr. and Mrs. Heister this morning, an older couple who were ailing, and Alice was more than happy to have the distraction to keep her mind off Caleb and his absence.

She put her pile of cards down on the table and exited the

back room into the main store; although, when she arrived, she wished she hadn't. There on the other side of the counter stood Cora and Sally Whitmer looking as smug as a pair of bugs in a warm rug. Alice suddenly wished she was still laid up in bed. "Can I help you ladies with something this morning?" she asked politely.

"We stopped by to pick up our dresses for the harvest social next weekend," Sally cooed.

"Of course," Alice said with a fake smile. "Will you excuse me for a minute," she said before turning and going back into the back room again to retrieve the dresses. She took a deep, calming breath before returning to the front of the store. "Here we are. If you'd like, you may try them on before you leave and make sure they fit right."

The girls smiled as they each took their dress and went to try them on in a little room at the other end of the store. Sally emerged first and sauntered over to the set of mirrors in the corner. "I absolutely adore it!" she squealed as she made a full circle while still admiring herself. "Cora, come out here!"

"I'm coming," the sister replied. "Oh, you look lovely," she said to her sister after she emerged from the room. "But don't I simply look divine?"

Alice felt physically ill having to listen to the girls dramatizing their good looks or rather the lack thereof. Personally, Alice thought the Whitmer sisters' sense of style was nonexistent and their physical appearances were nothing to boast about, but she wasn't about to tell them. Their tongues were sharp enough without being provoked, so she remained silent and waited for them to change back into their other dresses. "Will that be all for you two this morning?"

"Yes," Sally answered. "I believe Mother was already in here to pay for them."

"Yes, it looks like she did," Alice responded, seeing her pappy had written *paid* on the card attached to the dresses, indicating that payment had been received in full.

"Will we be seeing you at the social next weekend?" Cora

asked with a syrupy tone as Alice began to place the dresses in boxes for the girls.

"I'm not sure," Alice answered. "It depends on how I'm feeling."

"I understand," Sally said almost sympathetically. "You had quite an ordeal a couple weeks ago."

"Yes, you not only nearly drowned but you drove the handsome Mr. Newman back to the sea. I heard he is planning to never come back," Cora said with a sneer.

"He is planning to come back if he can but he isn't certain he'll be able to," Alice explained defensively.

"Oh, believe me. Where he's going, there's no coming back," Sally said before she and Cora left quickly with their new dresses in their arms.

Alice wanted nothing more than to throw her shoe at them. They were so hateful and mean. They made her blood boil. The gossip concerning Caleb's disappearance had reached an all-time high, which was undoubtedly where the Whitmer girls had learned their twisted version of the story. Caleb would tell her not to twist her petticoats over it but still, it made her angry. No one seemed to care that the last time he went to sea, he nearly died. No one seemed to care that she, Grace, and Augustus died a little more each day Caleb was gone.

Her eyes began to mist, and she went into the back room to finish her previous task. She had only been back there a few minutes, however, when the bell rang again. Alice almost stayed there but knew that was neither polite nor proper. So begrudgingly, she stood, wiped her eyes, put on her best fake smile, and went to the front of the store. She half expected to see the Whitmer sisters again but was delighted to see Betsy Winters standing there instead.

As Alice entered the store, Betsy's eyes lit up as she smiled, astonishing Alice. It was a rare moment indeed when Betsy Winters smiled, but her smile was contagious and Alice returned it eagerly. "You're looking well today, Mrs. Winters."

"Thank you," Betsy replied pleasantly. Alice had not seen

Betsy since she had been ill and by the way she looked, Alice would guess the illness had only done the woman good. She looked nearly ten years younger than her seventy-two years with her hair piled elegantly on top of her head and her dress freshly laundered and pressed.

"What brings you here today?" Alice asked as she walked around the counter and came to stand before the woman.

"Well, I brought in some paintings for you to take to the gallery," Betsy said, beaming.

"But . . ." Alice started, astonished by what she heard. "You said you needed a month to think it through."

"Well, I've thought it through, and I want you to take them today." Most days this statement would have been said with hostility and unpleasantness, but today it was said with friendliness and warmth. "Would you like to see them?" she asked with a mischievous twinkle in her eye.

"Oh, yes! Please!" Alice squealed as she rushed over to the door where Betsy had leaned the pictures against the wall. As Betsy took off the brown wrapping that protected the framed canvas, Alice stood in awe. This was a new painting, not one that had been in the room with the others. No. This was different. The colors were somehow brighter, the movements of the paint happier and the all around appearance of the painting was more pleasant than the ones Alice had seen at Betsy's home. "Oh, Betsy! It's beautiful!" she said as she looked at the exquisitely captured essence of the cherry grove that grew behind her grandparents' home.

"Since when have you taken to calling me Betsy?"

"I'm sorry . . . I . . . I . . ." Alice stammered, embarrassed that propriety had eluded her momentarily.

Betsy giggled and smiled. "Wait until you see the next one. I painted it several months ago. I just added a few finishing touches yesterday."

The second was a painting of the meadow outside of town. It was breathtaking! The greens were bright and happy while the flowers were soft and delicate. The river seemed to sing gleefully as it flowed along through the middle and Alice smiled at the little boy off to one side flying a kite. "It's wonderful! When did you have time to paint these?"

"I live by myself. What else do I have to do with my time?"

Alice giggled when she realized Betsy was only half-serious in her comment. "I'll take these down as soon as Nana and Pappy get back."

"Thank you," Betsy said with a smile. She turned towards the door but turned back to Alice as though she had forgotten something. "Miss Frank, I told you before that I don't want the money from these, correct?"

"Yes."

"Well, I've decided I'd like five percent to cover my costs of the canvases, frames, and paint. Then I want the rest split in half and half of it is to go to the gallery."

Alice smiled. Betsy turned and left the store before Alice had time to think that the woman had not specified where she wanted the other half to go. Quickly, she ran to the door to catch her but Betsy was already in the carriage and pulling away from the store. *My, she can move fast for an old woman,* Alice thought to herself as she took the paintings with her to the back room. She carefully replaced the brown wrapping around them and placed them in a corner, out of the way. Then she returned to her filing.

Several hours later, Henry and Gretchen entered the store, and Alice rushed from the back room to greet them. She stopped behind the counter though, as she saw the puzzled expressions of her grandparents. "What's that?" Henry asked as he pointed to something on the floor in front of the counter.

Alice moved out from around the other side. There leaning against the front counter sat something neatly wrapped in brown paper that was nearly three feet long and two feet tall. Alice momentarily wondered how it got there before she went to inspect it. The package had her name scrawled beautifully across the front, so she carefully picked it up and removed the brown paper. She gasped as the paper fell away and she viewed for the first time the masterpiece behind the paper. She was astounded that she had not seen the package earlier when Betsy was there, but she had been preoccupied with the two paintings the woman had given her to take to the gallery. A tear rolled down Alice's cheek as she gazed down at the beautiful painting she now held in her hands. The blues, greens, purples, pinks, and oranges made the most beautiful sunset over the ocean Alice had ever witnessed. The sunset seemed to glow. The artist had taken extreme precaution in commanding the waves of the ocean to demonstrate not only its danger but also its beauty.

Alice looked up briefly as Gretchen and Henry glanced over her shoulder at the painting. Then looking down again, she noticed a ship sailing on the horizon. Alice wondered whose ship was sailing through this masterpiece. Was it Neal's or Caleb's? No matter who it belonged to, Alice was touched that the woman would put so much thought and effort into this wonderful gift. A gift she would always cherish and one that held more meaning for her and Betsy than anyone else would ever imagine.

"That's beautiful, peach. Who's it from?" Gretchen asked.

"Summerlee Wynter," Alice whispered.

"Sure enough," Henry said as he pointed to the corner of the canvas where the name was beautifully woven into one of the waves. "I haven't seen one of her paintings in years. I wonder who gave it to you."

"I thought she died," Gretchen stated and Alice simply smiled.

"Oh, look here," Henry said as he bent down and picked up a white note off the ground. He looked it over and then handed it to Alice. "It looks like it's for you, peach."

Alice carefully set the painting on the counter before taking the note. She opened it to see the flowing script on the small card. Smiling, she read it through quickly to herself.

*Miss Frank,*

*I want the second half of the profits to go to Anthony Hielott for his shipyard. It was his granddaddy that Neal sailed for all those years ago and I want him to have the money. I hope your sailor comes home to you soon.*

*Summerlee Wynter*

Alice smiled as she folded the note and set it on the counter. Then picking up her painting, she went to the back room again. She marveled at the gift from Betsy as she tenderly placed the painting in the corner near the other two. Then she retrieved the other two paintings and walked back to the front of the store. "Do you mind if I take these to the gallery?" she asked her grandparents who still stood dumbfounded on the other side of the counter.

"Hold on there, peach," Henry said as he gaped at her. "Are those Summerlee Wynter paintings, too?"

"Yes."

"You know Summerlee Wynter?" Gretchen asked in disbelief and amazement.

"Yes."

"Since when?" Henry countered, also unbelieving.

"I discovered recently that I've known her for a very long time and never knew it. Summerlee Wynter is the painter's pseudonym," Alice explained.

"So why is she having you take care of her business?" Gretchen asked.

"She's afraid of rejection. That's why she quit painting all those years ago."

"How do you know so much when no one else even knew she lived around here?" Henry asked.

"I don't know if I can answer that question. She doesn't want people to know who she is," Alice answered honestly.

"Peach," Gretchen started, "I think if you are going to be involved with her, Henry and I deserve to know who she is and what you're up to."

Alice let out a loud, frustrated sigh. Gretchen was right. They had a right to know. Inwardly, Alice prayed Betsy would not be too upset. "You have to swear not to mention this to a soul."

After they nodded their assurance, Alice proceeded. "Summerlee Wynter is Betsy Winters. She paints under a pseudonym because her husband wouldn't let her sell her work," Alice explained.

"You're kidding," Gretchen laughed.

"No, I'm not," Alice said defiantly.

"What makes you so sure?" Henry said. "She's the bitterest woman I know."

"That's just the problem," Alice said, becoming frustrated. "That's the problem with everyone in this town. They can't see past the end of their noses to see the good in some people. They don't understand that usually something drives people to become like that. Most people aren't born sour. That's how it is with Betsy, too. And she doesn't want people to know who she is because that will tarnish all the good in the world that Summerlee Wynter has done." With that, Alice brushed past them quickly and left by way of the front door.

She was angry that her grandparents, of all people, were so quick to disbelieve in Mrs. Winters. Why weren't people willing to give the woman a second chance? She was a good person who had simply undergone more heartache in life than most. Securing the paintings tightly in her arms, Alice began to make her way to the gallery.

An hour later, she slowly made her way back to the store. The art gallery had been thrilled to have Summerlee Wynter paintings gracing their halls once more. Alice helped draw up a contract with them so she could act as mediator between Betsy and the gallery. She had met with Betsy outside the general store to tell her the good news. Betsy was, of course, as excited as Alice and people looked at the two with expressions of confusion and amazement as they passed. Alice slowly made her way back to the lions' den. She had been angry and snapped at her grandparents when she left, and now she began to dread the wrath she would inevitably face upon her return.

As she approached, she saw a wagon coming towards her at full speed. She leapt closer to the buildings as the wagon neared and was momentarily stunned when it stopped next to her.

Gretchen and Henry were in the front seat with anxiety on their faces. "Get in quickly!" Gretchen said as she motioned for Alice to join them. Uncertain what was happening, but knowing she didn't want to miss it, she quickly climbed into the back of the wagon.

"What's going on?" She asked once they were on their way again. She had to yell to be heard because of their fast pace.

"Augustus sent a rider into town with a note telling us they needed us down at the port immediately," Henry explained. "Evidently, everything is beginning to unfold although we don't know exactly what is going on."

Alice sat quietly yet felt anxious as they headed out of town. They made a brief detour to the Newman's home where Gretchen alighted. Alice began to follow but was stopped by Henry's hand on her shoulder. "I'm sorry, peach. You need to come with me," he said as the wagon lurched forward again.

"But why?" she asked nervously.

"Not sure exactly," Henry answered. "I was simply told to accompany you to port," he said with an apologetic look in her direction.

Alice began to feel more restless and uneasy as they approached the beach. It appeared to be completely empty except for Augustus and Anthony. Alice could feel the apprehension in the air as both men looked at her with worried faces. What was going on? Hopefully it had something to do with Caleb, but what? Moments later, the royal coach pulled up and Lawrence emerged. "Come on, peach," Henry said as he stood waiting to help her down.

"What's going on?" Alice asked.

"Hurry up you two," Lawrence said in a slightly hushed voice. "We need to get everyone in place." With that, he began to assign posts for each member of the group and before she had a chance to ask any questions, Alice was left alone with Anthony guiding her in the direction of the docks.

# Fourteen

When they finally stopped in front of the office, Alice asked, "What's going on?"

"From what I've gathered, no one knows for sure except Prince Lawrence. I guess he received word from Caleb that everything would be happening at dusk tonight. So here we are. Waiting for whatever dusk brings," Anthony said, apologizing for knowing so little about the circumstances, but Alice sensed he knew more than he told her.

Moments later, the door to the office burst open and Clarence came outside in a huff. Obviously upset about something, when he saw his father and Alice, he attempted a friendly, calm smile. "What are you two doing here?" he asked, a bit unnerved at their presence.

"We were merely talking and watching the sunset. Do you have a problem with that?" Anthony countered.

"Of course not. Why would I care if such a beauty decorated my beach?" he said with a smile at Alice.

"It isn't your beach, Clarence. It's mine, and I can write you off easily."

"Oh, I don't think so, old man," Clarence retorted. "That packet of papers I had you sign yesterday, stated that you turned your entire share of the company over to me. So, I own it all," Clarence said with a smug look. "You see, I have watched you over the years and know that you seldom read everything you sign. It was too easy," he said with a boisterous laugh. Reaching his hand out towards Alice, he pulled her by the arm away from his father. Alice panicked slightly and looked over her shoulder to Anthony, but he only smiled and nodded his head signaling everything would be all right.

"So," Clarence began once they were out of ear shot of his father. "I knew you'd come crawling back to me."

"I'm not crawling back to you."

"Oh, come now, Miss Frank," he said as he stopped and stood in front of her. "We both knew you'd never be able to stay away from me."

"What are you talking about? I only came down here to . . ." She was halted in her sentence by his repulsive and unwanted kiss. She pulled away and slapped him hard across the face. "I loathe you!" she yelled.

Clarence put a hand to his face where she had struck him, as though he expected to see blood from his face. Transferring his piercing gaze to Alice, her confidence instantly began to fade. The anger and fire she had been feeling moments before seemed to have been absorbed by his eyes. She looked at him in horror. His eyes danced with danger and foreboding. He glared at her and snarled, "No one gets away with striking me. But right now, I don't have time to play this game with you." Grabbing her violently by the arm he dragged her to the office. She did her best to keep up with his pace but he walked briskly and had an uncomfortable grip on her arm.

Reaching the office, he flung her at a chair before bolting the door and placing the key in his pocket. "What do you want from me?" she asked bravely as Clarence went to stand ominously behind his desk.

"The same thing I've always wanted," he said with a grin while he leered at her. A look crossed his face making her concerned he would make an advance towards her, but he quickly seemed to reconsider and went to a telescope near the big window behind his desk. Assuming he was looking for something on the ocean, she stood and quickly tried to think of ways she could escape his dominating presence, but he turned around before she was able to put any of her thoughts into action. Ever so slowly, he began making his way to her. She attempted to back up but found she had been backed into a corner of the small office. "I still want you. Tell me, Alice. Why do you hate me?" he asked quietly. Alice noted that if she did not know him, she might misinterpret his soft manner for being flirtatious and even almost sensuous.

Her senses began to muddle. She remembered when she first met Clarence. He was handsome, flirtatious, and constantly flattering her. Now as he stood before her, she once again saw those same qualities in him. She wondered if he had ever lost them or if she had simply grown immune to them. If Caleb had never returned, would she have still seen Clarence as the attractive man she once had?

She could not answer these questions and pushed them to the back of her mind in order to focus on the situation at hand. If she allowed him to proceed making his advance, her virtue would most likely be compromised. However, if she provoked him, she would certainly endure his wrath and possibly still face the same fate. She needed to make her decision quickly for he would surely grow impatient if she continued to remain silent.

"Oh, Clarence," she cooed softly and with as much bravery as she could muster. "You intimidate me, yes, but I don't hate you. We simply have different goals," she stated honestly as she reached a hand carefully to his face and caressed his smoothly shaved cheek ever so slowly. Clarence was thrown off by her reaction but recovered quickly as a greedy grin spread across his face. "But do you think I would entertain thoughts of having you right now?" she asked innocently as his smile faded briefly. "After all, the sun hasn't even set. Heaven knows who could happen in on us." She was playing the part of the dedicated lover well. All she needed to do was distract him and keep him at bay long enough for everything outside to unfold, whatever that was.

"I knew you loved me," he grinned triumphantly.

"Of course I do. But I certainly can't let anyone else in on that little secret, now can I? Where would the fun be in that?"

He backed up slowly but kept a watchful eye on her. "Would you care for some wine?" She nodded and he went to another room to retrieve the refreshment. She hoped that by sending him to the other room, it would procure the time she needed to discover what was going on.

Casually, but quickly, she made her way behind his desk to where his telescope sat and carefully looked through it. She gasped slightly as she saw two ships sailing on the horizon that grew steadily larger through the glass. One ship had white sails and one had sails with serpents. As Alice looked up from the glass she could see the ships in the distance, though they looked like one. The wheels in her head began to turn as her mind began to concoct all the possibilities of what this meant. Seeing the two ships together had obviously upset Clarence. The ship with the serpents on the sails was most likely the Silver Snake. The other ship looked like a Hielott & Son ship. So what were they doing together? Were they in business together or was the Silver Snake after the other ship? Was Caleb on the other ship or had he been captured by the Silver Snake? If he had been captured, was he dead or alive? And how would this affect Clarence?

The questions began to make her head pound so she sat in the chair behind Clarence's desk and looked out across the water, wondering briefly what had happened with Anthony, Henry, and the others. They would undoubtedly play roles in this evening's events, and she wished she were in the safety of her pappy's arms as opposed to this secluded domain with Clarence. Sitting back in the chair, she watched the sun set over the ocean. Tonight's sunset proved to be another beautiful tapestry of artwork that reminded her of Betsy's painting of the ocean. The two matched perfectly in Alice's mind.

Startled from her thoughts, she heard Clarence close and lock the door to the other room before coming into the main office with two wine glasses and a bottle of wine. "Watching the sunset?"

"Yes," Alice said with a satisfied smile. "It's beautiful tonight." Looking over the ocean again, she could see the two individual ships now, without the glass, which caused her anxiety to heighten slightly.

"I will never understand why you enjoy watching it so much. I always thought it was too dull a thing to waste my time on."

"Oh, but it's so romantic!"

"Well, if it makes you happy," he said. As he looked out over the water, a frown crossed his face but he wiped it off quickly, pulled her up from the chair, and wrapped his arms tightly around her. "Do you see those ships out there, Alice?"

"Yes."

"Well, one of them is mine and I need to meet it when it arrives. So what say you to having our little rendezvous before they get here?" he asked with a lecherous grin.

Alice smiled in an effort to detour him and lowered her voice. "Or . . . we could wait until after you've met them. I can stay here while you go out there and when you come back, I'll be right here," she said as she pushed away from him and sat back in his chair. "Waiting for you . . ." she trailed off in a whisper. She prayed she would live through the night with her honor intact but knew her performance had to be superb for Clarence to buy into it.

He grinned and set down the wine and glasses before approaching her, gathering her into his arms and exhausting her mouth with his intense and greedy kisses. She felt as though she would be sick from the repulsiveness of his kisses and she pushed him away, wondering again where her pappy had gone. With every ounce of courage she had, she smiled up at him sweetly and putting a hand to his chest said, "We must be patient, Clarence. If we get too excited, we'll get to rendezvousing now instead of later, and it will have to be over before we can even begin to enjoy it," she said referring to his engagement with the arriving ship.

Alice knew little about the intimate relations between a man and a woman. Her sole education on the matter was received from overhearing some young male servants at the palace talk of such things when she was younger. So, traversing blindly on what she had heard, she prayed that she did not sound too naïve and that she would not find out more on the subject by the hand of Clarence Hielott. At this point, she was certain he believed she did want to be with him. And for her safety, she needed him to continue thinking that way.

Instantly, the fire and anger returned to Clarence's eyes, and he roughly grabbed her arm and squeezed tightly as he pulled her up next to his body. "Why are you lying to me Miss Frank? What are you really doing here?" he growled dangerously.

Alice winced from the pain he was inflicting on her arm. "What are you talking about?" she questioned as innocently as possible.

"I know you don't love me, and you have never drunk wine before when I've offered it to you. Now what are you playing at?"

"I don't know what you mean," Alice cried. She tried desperately to pry his fingers off her arm.

"Something is going on. I can feel it. I know you're a part of it and I want to know what it is!" he yelled at her. "Tell me now, Alice!"

"I don't know! Honestly!" she cried. He threw her roughly against the desk.

"What do you know about Caleb's disappearance?" he growled with barely restrained anger.

"Nothing. I was unconscious when he left. All I know is that he left."

"Why?" Clarence yelled. Then he slapped her across the face.

"I don't know," she cried. The tears were streaming down her face and she was near total despair. He frightened her, for she had no information to offer that might spare her life. Instantly she wondered about everyone else that had been on the beach with her earlier. Where had they all gone? Could they not hear Clarence yelling at her? And where was Anthony? If she were not rescued by someone soon, she was afraid to think what might be her fate.

"What do you know of the missing sloop from my ship-yard?"

"I don't even know what a sloop is," Alice whimpered.

"Pull yourself together, Miss Frank! You are most unbecoming when you bawl like a baby," he said with disgust. "A sloop is a small boat. And you know nothing about it?"

"No," Alice whispered as she wiped the tears from her cheeks.

Clarence put a hand to his chin as he began to put the facts together. Alice watched him; the anger smoldered in his eyes as he glanced briefly at her. She tried to stand up straight and smooth out her skirt but winced in pain from being flung into the desk. Glancing over to where Clarence now stood, she quickly gazed out the window only to discover the two ships were quickly approaching the docks. Her anxiety heightened. What was Caleb planning for dusk? It was dusk now and in a matter of minutes the two ships would be anchored at the docks.

Clarence shoved Alice to the floor as he marched to the window for a closer look. Evidently, he had noticed the ships too. He angrily grumbled something under his breath, grabbed the full bottle of wine, and strode to the door leading from the office to the docks. "Time for me to go, Miss Frank," he said in a disgustingly syrupy tone. "You stay here and we'll have our little rendezvous upon my return. After all, you gave your word." An evil smile crossed his face before he left.

She heard a loud noise of something scraping across the porch and realized he had moved something heavy in front of the door. When she went over in an attempt to open it, she could barely budge it. Whatever Clarence had placed behind the door was far too heavy for her to move. She went to the window facing away from the ocean but was unable to get it to slide open even slightly. A smaller window sat on the other side of the office next to the large window facing the ocean. However, she quickly discovered it only opened enough to stick her hand through and for her to hear the waves crash against the shore. A realization hit her. There was no escaping Clarence

Hielott. So helplessly, she watched from the window as Clarence approached the docks and waited impatiently for the two ships to anchor.

It seemed like an eternity to Anthony Hielott, who stood in the shadows outside of the office, for the ships to pull into dock. It took every ounce of self-discipline he had to not burst into the office and tear the precious girl, Alice, from the monster, his own flesh and blood. Clarence continually tried to control Anthony, and it was time to put the boy in his place. This was Anthony's business, and he would not allow Clarence to run away with it and sell it piece by piece as he went. The only thing stopping him from rescuing the girl was his promise to Lawrence to wait and let things play out as planned. If particular events did not occur, everyone could be in serious trouble. One thing Anthony knew for certain was that if Caleb were dead or injured in any way, the deal with Captain Andress of the Silver Snake was off. The ordeal was stressful to say the least, but necessary.

Anthony's attention was arrested by the cries of joy erupting from sailors as they reached land. He watched the routine of duties run smoothly as the ship anchored. It had always been a joy to watch sailors emerge after a long journey. Over the past three years, he regretted allowing Clarence to take over and be the one to greet the sailors and pay them their wages. Now he was wiser and knew Clarence's motives. Nearly a year ago, Anthony became suspicious of Richard's strange behavior prior to the return of ships. He would frequently leave several weeks before a ship arrived and would escort them to shore.

In the past, Anthony had always thought it was to see to the ship's safe arrival. This was true to a point, but it was primarily to make sure the special cargo made it safely. Then Richard would sail out several days later with a small crew, only to return a month or two later. It always seemed strange at the time, but it all made sense now. Richard was the go-between man and it made Anthony's blood boil to realize the opium trading had been taking place directly under his nose. From what he guessed, Richard sailed out to oversee the drugs being transferred to the Hielott ship in the middle of the night and then left again a couple days later to see the drugs off to another ship.

As the sailors began to disperse, Anthony brought his attention back to the situation at hand. Knowing this ship contained a shipment of opium, he watched as the sailors filed off the ship with their belongings. Clarence handed out wages to the sailors who went on their merry way into town. They would be back in the morning to begin unloading the cargo—all but the opium. During this time, the Silver Snake hovered off shore about a quarter mile. She merely sat there. Waiting. Like a vulture waiting to attack its prey.

After nearly a half hour, the beach was clear again except for Clarence and Richard. Looking at the pair always put Anthony into a state of wonder. Richard, who was thick and tall, dwarfed Clarence. It always amazed Anthony that someone like Richard would take orders from a scrawny runt like Clarence.

They spoke now in hushed voices, but Anthony was close enough to hear the conversation and leaned forward slightly in order to catch every word. "I trust everything went as planned?" Clarence asked, taking one last sip of wine before tossing the bottle to the ground.

"Of course," came Richard's reply. "I expected no less."

"Then what are they doing here?" Clarence asked with irritation as he indicated to the other ship with a nod of his head.

"I'm not sure. All Captain Andress said was he wanted to escort us, to make sure nothing happened to us."

"What's that going to cost me?" Clarence said with a touch of disgust tainting his voice.

"Nothing."

"I don't believe that. Pirates always want something."

"I know. But he says he wants nothing from you. Just wants to keep an eye out for us. Keep us as an ally I guess."

"Hmmm," Clarence said as he rubbed his chin. "Did you get everything then?"

"The opium? Yes, sir. The Myrl has never let us down yet. They're good suppliers."

"Good. We'll unload at midnight."

"Why not now? No one's here."

"Because I have a tasty little morsel back in the office I need to. . . . What do you suppose they're coming to shore for?" Clarence said as he spotted a small boat of pirates heading their way.

"I don't know," Richard replied, looking out at the small boat, confusion written on his face. "They said they'd see us to safety and take off."

Clarence slapped Richard's head. "You never trust a pirate!" he exclaimed. "I'm starting to doubt your abilities and your loyalty."

"You know I'm completely loyal to only you," Richard growled. "I'd never cross you like that."

They waited in silence as the boat came ashore. Anthony half wished they would duke it out right then and there. The fight would have been no contest—Richard would have triumphed. Clarence was a pampered pansy. There was no way he would be able to defend himself against the other man.

"To what do I owe the pleasure, Captain Andress?" Clarence said as he approached the water. He had no smile on his face but he was affable.

"I merely wanted to make sure all's well with you and yer cargo," the tall, thin man stated as three other men came to stand behind him. One wore a large brimmed hat and the others wore scarves around their heads. All looked menacing and capable of inflicting bodily damage.

"As you can see, everything is fine. Did that concern truly require you to be accompanied by three henchmen?"

"That's a very bold jab comin' from a runt like you," the captain sneered.

"What do you want, Andress? If you've come for payment of some kind, I refuse to pay it. Richard here tells me you willingly offered an escort demanding no pay from me."

"That's correct."

"Then why have you come?"

"I've come for my pay, but not from you," the man said. "Ah, your highness," the captain said with only the slightest bow of his head.

Anthony turned, as did both Clarence and Richard, to see Lawrence making his way to the men. "Right on time I see, Captain Andress," Lawrence said.

"Yes, sire. An' the package is intact."

"Thank you. I believe this will more than compensate you and your men for your efforts," Lawrence said as he handed the captain a pouch.

The captain opened it enough to expose a large amount of both paper money and coins. He smiled. "This'll do nicely," he said with a slight bow of his head. "If you're ever in need of anythin' again, don't hesitate."

"I won't. Thank you!" Lawrence said. He handed the man a folded piece of parchment before he retreated, leaving Clarence and Richard in a state of shock.

The captain placed the unread parchment in his coat pocket and then turned with his men and headed back to the small boat. Only then did Clarence finally regain his composure and stop the men. "May I ask you something?" When the men turned, Clarence continued. "What package did you deliver to the Prince? I see nothing."

Captain Andress smiled and said maliciously, "You."

"Me? I don't understand," Clarence said slowly.

"O' course you don't," the captain said with an evil smile. "You see, I hold all the cards here in this round."

"Like what?" Clarence countered.

"Like me," the man with the large brimmed hat said as he stepped forward. Richard and Clarence exchanged looks of bewilderment before the man slowly pulled off his hat. Their expressions quickly turned to disbelief and rage while Anthony only smiled. The man under the hat was none other than Caleb Newman.

# Fifteen

As Alice watched the scene unfold before her, she breathed a sigh of relief as she saw Caleb. She had not recognized him before with his wide brimmed hat, his clothes looking amazingly worn, and his face covered with over a week's growth of facial hair. He looked scruffy and dangerous. His hair, she realized, had not been trimmed since he had come home, and now it looked a little scraggly tied at the back of his head. His eyes were full of hatred and venom, and he wore an almost evil grin on his face. The overall uncharacteristic look which he sported somehow had Alice staring unabashedly at him. He was so handsome, even in his current state.

Circumstances allowed her little time to ponder on his good looks, for she instantly became aware that smoke swept through the office. She glanced over her shoulder and saw the drapes on fire. Looking around for what might have caused the fire, she saw a candle had tipped over by an open window on the other side of the office. She thought for certain that the drapes on the far side of the office had been pulled closed before and she had been unable to open the window. Now the window stood open, the drapes were also opened, and fire spread quickly all around her. She ran for the door but failed in her attempt to push it open. Quickly she ran to the open window but stopped halfway there. Her body proved unwilling to pass through the burning flames to get to the open window. She looked around the room in a panic. Time was quickly running out. The flames consumed everything at an alarming speed. She needed to escape! She ran again to the window behind the desk. Pushing on it as hard as she could, she was still unsuccessful in opening it any further.

She began to cough as the smoke intensified by the minute. Quickly, she dropped to the floor where there wasn't quite as much smoke so she could get a little better breath. Then, holding her breath and standing, she reached for a chair. She attempted to pick it up, but the room only contained a few over-sized leather chairs, and they were far too heavy for her petite frame to lift. Frantic, she looked around for anything she might be able to pick up and throw through the window. An ink barrel simply made a mess, the empty wine glasses shattered, scattering glass all over the floor while the window remained intact. The drawers were locked and nothing else lay on the desk. Not even a picture. She dropped to the floor again and began to panic. Gasping for air, she was certain she was going to die. There was no way for her to get out. Clarence had locked the door to the back room and she was now a prisoner. She screamed before she was thrown into a coughing fit and consciousness began to evade her until she finally succumbed to her fate.

"What are you doing here?" Clarence sneered at Caleb. "Why don't you go back to your ship and your own kind, Pirate? I don't want your kind of filth on my beach." At these comments, the pirates who stood behind Caleb grumbled and moved towards Clarence in an advancing fashion until Caleb put a hand up to halt them and they obeyed.

"Happy to see me?" Caleb scoffed. "Well, you should be." Clarence and Richard each took a step backward as Caleb and the pirates behind him took slow yet determined steps forward. About that time, Henry, Augustus, and Lawrence appeared to make their presence known and block off any retreat route Clarence or Richard might attempt.

Clarence looked around in panic but gained control quickly. "And why is that? Are you planning to feed me to the sharks or some other piratey punishment? You've got nothing on me, Newman."

"Oh?" Caleb said scornfully. "So, I suppose if a couple of my comrades went aboard your ship here, you'd have nothing to hide."

The color drained from Clarence's face moments before it burned red with hatred. "What do you want, Newman? Just say the word, then I'll leave you alone, and you leave me alone like two upstanding citizens."

"Upstanding citizens?" Caleb said with a smirk while he turned to look at the pirates behind him. "Didn't he just call me a pirate?" As the other pirates chuckled maliciously and nodded their heads, Caleb turned back around to Clarence, who had retreated a bit further from him. "You should know, Hielott, pirates don't play fair. And since that's what I am, as you so kindly reminded me, that rule applies to me too," he said with an evil smile. "Now, I want you to leave the little cherry tart alone, because she's mine. Next, I want you and your scummy pal here to unload that opium you've got hidden on board. And finally, I'll let you have a choice of what you want to do next."

Clarence seemed to gain a little confidence at Caleb's last statement. He straightened noticeably and smoothed his vest with his hands. "I have no idea what you're talking about. Opium? On my ship! Ridiculous! You need to do your research better before you start accusing a man, Newman," he said with a sidewise glance at the prince.

Lawrence rolled his eyes and Caleb simply laughed. "You have nerve, I'll give you that. Don't you want to know what your choices are?"

"No, but why don't you humor me," Clarence sneered.

"I will," Caleb growled with all evidence of mirth abolished instantly. "You can go quietly with Prince Lawrence. I'm sure they have a pleasant little cell in the dungeons for you. Or . . ." he paused for dramatic effect as a grin spread across his face, "you can come with us and we'll teach you all about those 'piratey' punishments."

Laughter erupted from Clarence causing everyone around him, including Richard, to look at him in surprise. "You really don't think I can be had that easily do you?" Clarence asked.

Before Caleb could respond, Clarence placed a fist quickly in Caleb's face followed by a foot planted squarely in his groin. Caleb doubled over in pain as the pirates behind him tore into Richard and Clarence. Caleb took the opportunity to look around at the others in his company. Lawrence stood on alert, ready to take action at any moment. Henry and Augustus stood at their posts appearing stunned and in shock at what they were witnessing. Caleb had expected as much. He was a different person when he was with members of the Silver Snake. Playing the bad guy tonight had been easy. He'd learned the part well during his five years sailing on the Silver Snake and now it seemed to be paying off.

Glancing around again, he expected to see Anthony and was disappointed by his friend's absence. The next instant, Caleb saw a shadow stumble out of the office that seemed to suddenly be producing an abundance of smoke. As the figure came out of the shadows and into the light of the night, Caleb recognized the man as Anthony carrying a small lifeless body in his arms. For a moment, Caleb wondered who the small person was. It looked like it could be a young boy, but the body wore heavy skirts. Suddenly, in the light of the fire which now began to roar with intensity from the building behind them, Caleb saw the dancing copper flames of the girl's hair.

Instantly Caleb jumped to his feet. He hollered for the other men to take Richard but leave Clarence alone. Then he walked over to where Clarence lay holding his nose on the ground. Caleb bent over and grabbed the front of Clarence's shirt, easily but angrily pulling him to a standing position. "How dare you imprison her and then set the place ablaze," Caleb growled menacingly at the man. He kept his overwhelming anger in check by lowering his voice, so that only Clarence could hear the death dripping from it.

"Wh . . . What are you talking about?" Clarence stammered.

"Alice. What did you do to her?" Caleb said with a bit more volume.

Clarence smiled as the advantage shifted. "That's for me to know and you to die wondering."

"You're a coward and a thief, Hielott," Caleb thundered. "Captain, tie up that whelp and unload the ship. Then I'll let you take this coward and do what you want to him," Caleb said with a sinister smile.

"I thought you said I got to choose," Clarence said with panic edging his voice.

"You took too long." Caleb smiled. "And don't worry. I'll be there with them to make sure you don't get off."

"But I thought we were friends," Clarence whined.

"Save your breath, Hielott. You and I both know that's a lie. Now silence your mouth before I do it for you," Caleb said as he thrust the broken man to the ground.

"You should have seen how she pleaded with me to touch her," Clarence said as Caleb began to turn away from him.

"You're a liar."

"Don't you wish? Believe me when I tell you her kiss revealed it all."

Caleb lost his temper. Picking up Clarence with one fist, he sent the liar sprawling in the sand with the other. He walked over to his unconscious adversary and said with low growl, "Nobody makes light of intimate relations with a woman in my presence, especially relations with Alice." Then expelling the rest of his anger, he kicked Clarence brutally in the side making the unconscious man groan and everyone present cringe at the sound of his cracking ribs.

Turning, Caleb watched as Henry and Augustus finished tying up Richard and moved over to tie up Clarence. Looking over at the ship, he saw that Lawrence, Captain Andress, Crane, and Holden were unloading the opium from the ship. Nodding in assurance to himself that everything was going well, he began to walk over to where Anthony sat holding Alice. "What happened?" Caleb asked when he reached the pair.

"Yesterday, Clarence made me sign some papers giving my estate and business over to him. I signed it to appease him and not make him suspicious. I had every intention of destroying the papers but didn't have the opportunity until tonight. Clarence placed a couple hundred pound barrels in front of the door making it almost impossible to get into the office undetected by him, so I went to the window. You know the one that only opens from the outside. Well, I bumped my head trying to climb in and it took me a minute to come back to my senses. I must have knocked over a candle or something because when I looked up, the place was ablaze." Anthony looked down at Alice before he finished. "She couldn't get out and by the time I finally got them barrels moved, she'd already passed out."

Both men looked down lovingly at the lifeless form of Alice cradled in Anthony's arms. She looked peaceful, and Caleb regretted putting her through everything tonight. She had seemed to be a great candidate to help and apparently she had gotten Clarence's blood racing before Caleb arrived, which had proved to be a positive asset. He squatted next to Anthony and gently wiped the ash from her face with a handkerchief from his pocket. Then he gently kissed her still lips. As though it were a fairy tale, her eyes began to flutter and then open slightly before a thin smile appeared on her face.

"Hello, beautiful," he whispered. "How do you feel?" She opened her mouth to speak, but her whispers were raspy and barely audible, let alone understandable. "Shh. It's okay. I'm just glad you're all right." She smiled at him as a tear rolled down her blackened face. "Did he hurt you, sugar?" She slowly rocked her head back and forth once in a negative fashion. Caleb breathed a sigh of relief and smiled at her. "Good. I'm sorry you got stuck in the middle of all this." Again Alice attempted to speak but Caleb placed a finger lightly on her lips. "Save your strength, sugar. I've a feeling you'll need it."

"Why?" Anthony butted in. "Do you think something will happen to her?"

"No. At least I hope not. But I have to go back with them and I want her in good health if I ever return."

"What do you mean, *if*?" Anthony said with a disapproving look on his face.

"I mean, I don't know if I'll be back," Caleb said matter-of-factly. "I pray that I will but I just don't know."

"Where're you going?" Anthony asked.

"I have to go back to the Silver Snake. Last time I left with five days of my service left to serve. As a result, I'm at their disposal if they wish."

"But you made them all very wealthy men."

"I know, but they're pirates," Caleb said as he returned his gaze back to Alice. "I'm sorry, sugar, but I have to go. I can't spend the rest of my life running. I just can't." He watched as another tear escaped onto her cheek. He leaned forward, placed a light kiss on her still lips, stood, and walked back to the beach.

"That was a noble thing you did, Caleb. I commend you for it," Lawrence said looking back to the ship.

Caleb looked down as sadness overtook him. "I don't know if it was worth the trouble."

"What makes you say that?"

He shrugged his shoulders. "I just can't bear to leave her again," he said with a glance over at Alice, still held protectively in Anthony's arms.

"Don't worry. You'll see her again." Caleb looked at him skeptically. "Lillian wouldn't have it any other way," Lawrence said with a wink. The two men embraced momentarily before Henry and Augustus appeared to say their good-byes.

Henry silently shook Caleb's hand before Augustus embraced him in an affectionate hug. "Be strong, son," Augustus said with a sad smile. Then Caleb retreated to the boat with Captain Andress, Holden, Crane, and the two prisoners.

The weeks and months that passed after the episode on the beach went by slowly and with little incident. Alice recovered from the fire within a day or two and put all her energy into helping her grandparents at the store. She missed Caleb miserably but also knew that if she were to dwell on his absence she'd go insane.

In the ten months since his departure, life had taken on a familiar routine. Alice helped Henry with the early morning chores before going to the store for several hours to do filing, cleaning, sewing, or whatever else needed done. She would then head home to start supper, and then work on needlepoint or read a book in the evening. Several days a week she would stop in and see her mother briefly only to return to the monotonous rituals of her life. On her way home from the store in the late afternoon, she always stopped by to pick up the post. Day after day, she was forced to squelch the disappointment that filled her bosom at the absence of any correspondence from Caleb.

Today proved to be no different. As she thumbed through the post she saw letters addressed to Henry and one to Gretchen. The last one, however, caught her attention. On the front of the envelope in immaculate script it read,

*To: Henry & Gretchen Lind and Alice Lind Frank.*

Curious, Alice quickly lifted the seal and withdrew a single card.

*Your presence is cordially requested at the palace
to honor a man who has displayed
both courage and sacrifice for his entire kingdom.*

*The ball will be held tomorrow evening at 6 o'clock.*

An unexpected chill ran down her spine as she read the card. She had been to many royal balls as a servant but now she was invited as a guest. Her heart jumped into her throat as she fought to keep her emotions at bay. She was touched that she would be on the guest list yet uncertain whether she should accept the invitation. The unfamiliarity of being on this side of the festivities stalled her excitement. Also, attending a social gathering of this magnitude would undoubtedly surpass her comfort zone.

Later that evening as she sat in the parlor with her grandparents, she could feel the eyes of both Henry and Gretchen boring into her. Uneasy as she was, she continued to work on her needlepoint not looking up at either of them. There had been a heated discussion just before dinner about the ball, at which time Alice adamantly stated that in no uncertain terms would she be attending. She told them she did not like all the pomp and circumstance but in truth she could not endure her memories from previous balls. She was convinced that if she were to attend, her heart would burst with emotion, and her life would abruptly come to an end.

Finally, her grandfather cleared his throat and broke the silence that hung ominously in the air. "I think it would be good for all of us to go to the ball as a family," he said in a dominating tone.

Alice looked at him in warning but he put up his hand to stop her protests. "Now before you get your tail feathers in a knot, let me finish." He looked over at Gretchen, who nodded her head in support while Alice rolled her eyes in frustration. "There will be many nice young men there and I think it's time you moved on. Caleb may never come back, peach. You can't be waiting for him your entire life. You'll miss too much."

"Perhaps I don't mind. And besides, he's come back before. Even after years of everyone thinking he was dead, he came back."

"But, peach," Gretchen soothed. "He willingly went back to the Silver Snake with a price on his head. Do you honestly think even he could make it out alive without a miracle?" Alice's head fell forward, and she stared at nothing in particular while her hands played with the loose string from her needle work. "Now, I don't mean to depress you, peach, but I think it's about time you went to a social function. Who knows, you might even have fun," Gretchen said. Alice could hear the smile in her voice.

Alice had no desire to go, but it was becoming evident that she may not have a choice. Thinking about living a life without Caleb made her tired. So, putting a brave smile on her face, she looked up sadly and said, "I'll think about it." That seemed to please her grandparents for the time being, so she picked up her needlepoint and said, "I'm going to bed. Good night." She then proceeded to her bedroom as the murmur of good nights trailed behind her. Her last conscious thought before she slipped into a fitful slumber was, *"If I make it through tomorrow,* that *will be a miracle."*

The evening of the ball arrived and Alice could feel the butterflies fluttering madly in her stomach. She felt a little out of sorts wearing the nicest dress she'd ever owned and sitting on a blanket in the bed of her grandparents' old wagon. Wearing a dress of the softest blues, she felt like royalty. Gretchen had made it for her and given it to her this morning. She hadn't said but Alice suspected Gretchen had known about the ball months in advance.

As they pulled up in front of the palace, Alice's breath caught in her throat. The evening was cloudy but for some reason she felt as though she were entering a fairy tale. The lights in the palace danced with the elegance of a thousand diamonds. The smell of wild flowers tickled her nose. She watched as people streamed into the palace on the red carpet that had been rolled out to the carriages and wagons. Only then did she realize the entire kingdom had been invited. Everyone wore their nicest clothes; some wore more expensive attire than others, but everyone attended.

Taking Henry's hand, she alighted from the wagon and gave her pappy a nervous smile. "It'll be all right, peach. You'll see," Henry reassured her.

Suddenly a man around her own age appeared at her side and extended his arm to escort her to the festivities. She smiled at him, accepted his arm, though somewhat tentatively, and allowed him to lead the way to the courtyard where a large dance floor had been erected to accommodate the many dancers. When they arrived, the young man left to escort some other dateless beauty, and Alice had a brief moment to marvel at the simple elegance of the decorations. She felt as though she had entered a magical, romantic wonderland. Alice had arrived exactly on time with her grandparents and just as they walked through the archway leading to the courtyard, the first song began and couples made their way to the dance floor. A smile found its way to her face as Henry led Gretchen to the floor, but Alice suddenly felt very lonely.

Looking around for someone she might know, she spotted a door leading to the kitchen. Quickly, she made her way to the door. As she was about to enter, a servant stopped her. "Is there something you need, miss?"

"Oh, no, thank you. I was simply looking for my mother," she said with a smile. Then she proceeded through the door.

Upon her entrance, the entire kitchen staff turned in her

direction. Many of them Alice knew and others she didn't. The ones who knew her smiled, and one pointed to a corner where her mother, covered in flour, was busily decorating some fresh pastries. Hearing the commotion, Theresa turned and let out a gasp as she beheld her daughter. "Come here, peach." Alice approached the woman and gave her a big hug, ignoring the flour that would inevitably cling to her lovely gown. "I didn't know you'd be here."

"I didn't want to come, but Nana and Pappy dragged me."

"And from the looks of that gown, I'd say you probably came kicking and screaming the entire way," Theresa said sarcastically with a smile while her daughter threw her a playful scowl. "You look lovely, peach."

"Thank you," Alice said, "although I must confess it feels weird to be on that side of the door instead of this side."

"Now you don't let that bother you," Theresa scolded. "I want you to go out there and have a good time. And who knows," she said with a glint of mischief in her eye. "Maybe you'll find the man of your dreams out there."

"I doubt that," Alice said skeptically.

"Well, I need to get back to work, so give me a hug," Theresa said as she gathered her daughter into her arms once more. Then, holding Alice away from her and smiling, she said, "You look like a dream, peach."

With that, Theresa turned back to her work, and Alice had little choice but to return to the party. As she exited the door, a young man with blond hair approached her and asked her to dance. She graciously accepted, though her heart seemed to break with every step. With each new song she danced with a new man, all of whom were very attentive to her, but she could not seem to pull her heart and mind away from Caleb.

Finally, she broke free from the young men for a moment and went to get a glass of punch before meandering to an archway at the edge of the courtyard where few people were. From here she could see the entire city below bordered by a vast meadow in one direction and the ocean on the other. The sight was spectacular. At that moment, she noticed the clouds disappearing and the stars beginning to shine brightly down on the party. A tear escaped onto her milky skin, and she quickly brushed it away. She missed Caleb so horribly. Last summer at the town social, it had been Caleb who had sought her out to cheer her up and ask her to dance. Now, she simply stood alone with her memories. Again.

Suddenly she heard a throat being cleared from behind her. She turned around, startled, and a smile graced her face as she beheld Anthony Hielott. He smiled at her and said, "I know I'm old enough to be your daddy, but would you do me the honor of a dance?"

"Certainly," she said with a smile and allowed him to escort her to the dance floor. When they began to dance she asked, "How's the new office?"

"Great! You know if it hadn't been for you, I don't know what I would've done."

"It wasn't me," she reminded.

"I know. But I don't know who else to thank. So I hope you pass on the thanks."

"I will."

After the night on the beach when the office burned down, Betsy Winters had been true to her word. When her paintings began selling, she took her five percent from the earnings and then divided up the rest between the gallery and Hielott & Son. Alice delivered the money to Anthony and told him it was a donation from an anonymous source. She prayed that some day Betsy would allow people to know it was *her* paintings that so many people loved—but perhaps in time. Betsy had already begun opening up and becoming friendlier with the entire community, and Alice believed the woman even had a few friends.

"Alice, I'm sorry if my son ever hurt you in any way," Anthony said, breaking into her thoughts.

"Thank you, but we've had this conversation before," she said smiling at the man. "It's forgotten."

"I know, but I still . . ."

Just then, the song ended and everyone began clapping.

Gradually the crowd quieted and watched as a man stood on a tall podium and cleared his voice. "Gentlemen and ladies of the court, please welcome your hosts: his highness, Lawrence Christopher Phelps, and her highness, Lillian Hazel Phelps."

The crowd parted and bowed as the prince and princess walked to the podium, arm in arm. Alice smiled. They were such a lovely couple—so happy and so obviously still in love. As they reached the podium the crowd stood and waited in anxious excitement for the announcement of their honored guest. Lawrence spoke first and as he did, Alice became acutely aware of the nerves that suddenly assaulted her.

"Thank you all for coming. It is a beautiful evening and I hope everyone is having a wonderful time." At this, the crowd applauded approvingly before Lawrence continued. "I would first like to excuse my father as he has taken very ill this evening." He paused only momentarily before continuing. "As you all know, we are holding this celebration in honor of a very special man. He has endured much to serve me and the land he loves. These past many months he has been on a top secret mission to protect this land from war. He has journeyed hundreds of miles and has completed his mission successfully. He is an upstanding citizen and a wonderful man."

Lawrence glanced down at his wife and smiled. Lillian's eyes filled with tears and the emotion in her voice was evident when she spoke. "Now, it is my privilege to introduce to you our honored guest and my beloved cousin, Caleb Joseph Newman."

Alice stood in stunned silence, dumbfounded as she slowly turned and saw Caleb walking with the authority of a king towards the podium where his cousin and her husband stood. As he approached, he threw Alice a wink which brought her back to reality. She shook her head briefly and a giant smile spread across his face.

Dressed in a black suit with a red sash across his chest, he had the appearance of a well-respected gentleman. His sun-bleached hair was combed back and trimmed to a neat length once again, and his skin was dark and golden from the many months he had spent at sea, yet what impressed Alice most about his appearance was his smile and the twinkle in his eye. He had obviously found peace within himself and his life.

He reached the podium and bowed on one knee in front of the royal couple. At that moment, Lawrence withdrew a sword from a pillow held by a servant directly behind him. He then held it vertical in the air in front of him. "Caleb Joseph Newman, by the power vested in me by my father, King Christopher Mortimer Phelps, and by all these witnesses here, I hereby dub thee, Sir Caleb Joseph Newman." The crowd exploded in an uproar while Alice simply stood frozen in place watching the events unfold before her. As the crowd continued to make their approval known, Caleb rose and embraced both Lawrence and Lillian in turn before bowing to the audience. Once the commotion died somewhat, Lawrence took his wife's hand, led her to the dance floor, and began dancing with her as the music began again. Alice watched with a smile as they floated gracefully around the floor.

Just then, she felt a hand on her shoulder. She turned to see Caleb standing behind her. He bowed dramatically and offered his hand to her. She took it nervously and allowed him to lead her around the floor. It was everything she could do to keep her feet moving in the appropriate fashion. No matter how hard she tried, she could not stop staring into his handsome face. This felt like a dream, being here in his arms and dancing before the entire kingdom.

"Stop staring, sugar. It's rude," he whispered with a chuckle.

Instantly she returned to her senses. "Don't you reprimand me," she scolded softly. "I haven't heard from you in ten months and then you show up and are knighted, and I'm supposed to know exactly how to react? Well, I'm sorry but I don't."

His expression became less merry and he looked around. The dance floor was now full of happily dancing couples. Stopping, he took her hand in his and led her out to the arch overlooking the city where she had been standing earlier. He remained silent until they were just outside the archway. "I'm sorry I never wrote, sugar. But I couldn't. If the letter was intercepted . . . if anyone knew I was alive or what I was doing. . . . I'm so sorry." His apology was sincere and at that moment she felt nothing towards him but love. He had come home to her and nothing else mattered.

Still, she had one more question to ask. "What happened after that night?"

"I returned to the Silver Snake. Originally, they wanted to take my life but I took them ashore, made them wealthy men, and gave them two prisoners in my place. Lawrence knew that alone would not be enough to save me. He knew it would take care of Clarence Hielott and put me in better standings with the pirates, but it did not guarantee me my life. So he commissioned them to be privateers and for the past ten months we have been doing things to help Lawrence prevent war with some of our neighbors. Anyway, finally a month ago, Lawrence contacted the Silver Snake and released them from their service, paid them a very handsome sum, and demanded that I be returned safely. Upon my safe arrival, they received a second installment, and now here I am."

Alice stood in wonderment at what she was hearing. "All this time. . . . Did anyone else know?"

"No."

"When did you arrive?"

"Yesterday morning."

"Why didn't you . . . ?" Alice started in frustration. "Do you know how much I've worried? Do you know how long I've . . . ?"

"Shhh," Caleb said as he put a finger to her lips. "I'm sorry but I wanted to surprise you."

"Surprise me? With what? The fact that you're still alive and the last ten months that I've endured heartbreak were unnecessary? Or—" Her ranting was cut short as he pulled her to him and administered a much longed for kiss. The taste of him was delicious to her and her frustration melted almost instantly in his passionate embrace. She wasted no time in allowing her arms to wrap around him in welcomed affection.

When they finally broke apart, he kept his arms at her waist.

"I'm sorry, Alice. But I wanted to wait until tonight to see you. To tell you how much I love you." Her mouth dropped open at his revelation. "It's true. And the last ten months have been the worst of my entire life. I wanted nothing more than to be here with you. I love you so much. You are my life. You are my breath. My ocean. I nearly went crazy without you. I need you and I don't want to live a day longer than I have to without you as my wife."

Alice was stunned into silence. She simply stared at him as though he was out of his mind. "Well, say something, sugar."

"I don't know where to start," she mumbled.

"Start by telling me you'll marry me. Here. Tonight. Before any more time passes."

"Tonight? But where would we live? What would our families think?"

Caleb chuckled. "Once I got back yesterday, I purchased some land with a decent sized house near my folks and signed on as a partner with Anthony. And as for our families, I met with your grandfather this morning and he has given us his permission and his blessing."

"But what about my mama?"

"Why don't you ask her?" he said.

Slowly she turned around and saw her mother emerge from the archway a little ways away. "Mama?" Alice asked.

"You would be a fool not to marry him, peach. He's a wonderful man and I look forward to the grandchildren the two of you will give me," Theresa said with a smile before she hugged her embarrassed daughter. "Your father would have been proud of this choice if he were still here," she whispered.

"Well, what do you say, sugar? Will you marry me?"

She turned around and saw that he had gotten down on one knee and held his hand out to her. Tears began to run down her cheeks and she rushed into his arms. "Yes! Yes, yes, yes!" she exclaimed. He picked her up and twirled her around. Moments later Alice heard sniffles and looked around to see that Grace, Augustus, Henry, Gretchen, Anthony, Lawrence, and Lillian had all joined Theresa. "This is unreal," Alice muttered as she witnessed all these people who loved her so much.

"Well, Pa. Why don't you fetch Pastor Jones and we'll get this show on the road," Caleb said with a grin.

Alice looked to Caleb in question. "We're really going to get married tonight?"

Caleb chuckled. "Yes. Why? Are you having second thoughts?"

"Oh, no! It's just . . ."

"Is it because I'm a sailor and a pirate? That I'm a knight? Or that by being those things I'm now incredibly wealthy?"

Alice pulled herself together. "No. I just can't believe you would want me."

"Oh, I want you, sugar," he said with a smile.

"And you won't go to sea again?" she whispered, afraid to look up at him. "I couldn't handle losing you again."

"My love is yours, sugar. I'll always stay by your side," he whispered. Then lifting her chin so that her eyes met his, he asked, "So, will you have me? Here? Tonight?"

"Yes," she whispered through her tears. "Yes, and you will be mine forever," she smiled and kissed him with a passion that was overwhelming. In the past half hour, she had gone from enduring immense heartache to having the love of her life reappear and ask to spend the rest of his life with her. It was like a dream. An unexpected dream, but a lovely dream all the same. Her love for him was as vast and deep as the ocean was blue. And never again would she lose him to the sea. His love would be hers forever.

1. What, if any, are the similarities between Alice Lind Frank and Betsy Winters? Between Alice and Grace Newman?

2. What are some lessons Alice learns from Grace?

3. What consequences or blessings did Betsy acquire as a result of her marriage?

4. What are the differences in morals between Betsy and Alice?

5. Why was Caleb so determined to keep his piracy a secret? Could he have avoided or gained anything by telling anyone upon his return?

6. What kinds of emotional damage did Alice endure after the death of her father?

7. What kind of influence has Theresa Frank been in her daughter's life?

# About the Author

Plunged into a musical family at birth, Rachel Rager was exposed to the excitement and magic of musical theater throughout her childhood. Starry-eyed, she attended college musical rehearsals with her pianist mother, imagining herself as the heroine in the spotlight. She was a hopeless romantic from the start. Rachel's own musical gifts motivated her through college, and she now holds a vocal performance degree in operatic singing. She has loved writing romance novels for over six years. Creative writing has served as a beautiful escape from the emotional rigors of raising her family.

Rachel currently lives in Casper, Wyoming with her handsome husband—the love of her life. There she enjoys curling up by a blazing fire with a good book, getting her own creative thoughts on paper, and singing until the coyotes start howling. She also loves picnics in the park and being a mom to three future starlets.